Sex Addiction

Fist Publication 2018

Published in the United States by
BirrowsINK LLC

Editor: Laurielle Noël

BURROWSINK
Publishing

Also by Ainsley Burrows

Novels

Bang Bang Bang: A Summer Of Sin In Brooklyn
Children Carrying The Sky

Books of Poetry

Black Angels With Sky-Blue Feathers
The Woman Who Isn't Was
The Wolf Who Cried Boy
The Spellcaster's Manual

Photography & Poetry

Street Pigeons

thank you
Laurielle Noël

to all the lovers who make brooklyn move.

Sex Addiction

A Novel

by Ainsley Burrows

Chapter One

He never thought in a million years this could ever happen to him. How did he get to this point? His brain was racing. It was sad really. Here he was, a high-powered lawyer, on his back on the floor of his bathroom with one hand in the air, trying to stop one of his best friend's from plunging a knife into his chest.

"Maurice no!" Sophie screamed.

"Ahhhhhhhh!" Max gave out a sound so primal the paint on the walls shivered.

Maurice's eyes were two balls flushed with hatred and vengeance, he gritted his teeth and slammed the knife into Max. Max grabbed his chest as everything went black. It was painless. He felt nothing. Was this what death felt like?

One second later Max slowly opened his eyes, strangely this took more energy than he expected. At first, he thought he was dreaming again but he was not sure. Then a wave of pain washed over his body. His everything ached. He started saying a prayer in his head. *Dear god, please, please, please, please let this be a dream*, he kept repeating to himself.

When he eventually managed to open his eyes everything was blurry, everything was heavy. He waited a few seconds; *and Bang*.

His entire face and chest were like the undercarriage of a building, with tubes and hoses and pipes running every which way in and out of his face and neck and stomach.

"What the fuck!" He screamed as he anxiously started snatching the hoses and tubes from his face and body.

He was shaking. His body covered in a cold sweat. His hospital room door swung open and two nurses rushed in and grabbed his arms and tried to calm him down. He fought as hard as he could.

"Honey are you ok?"

Max opened his eyes a second time and looked up at Sophie's troubled face.

"What?" He said viciously as he collected his thoughts.

He exhaled aggressively. She could feel the tension leave his body.

"I, I –I'm good," Max had a troubled look on his face.

He had been having nightmares about the Amanda situation for the entire year now.

Sophie knew he was lying. She kissed him gently on his forehead. Then on his lips, then his chest, then she moved her kisses gently down his torso. She took her time because she wanted him to want it. She kept kissing the area just between his torso, pelvis and thigh. It was as if she was slowly torturing him.

He was writhing with wanting by the time she got the tip of his dick between her lips. Her sweet mouth was just what he needed. She had become somewhat of an expert at reading exactly what he wanted. She worked his dick for a while, kissing and slurping until it was glistening, before she mounted him slowly and fucked the nightmares out of him.

She watched his eyes intently as she rode him. She paid close attention to his hands. She met his stroke at every corner, every twist, every turn. She fucked him as if she had personally met every cell in his body, as if they were one person. Their movement was high art. She held her climax. She waited for him. And when the intensity grasped his face, she rode him harder and faster. When he sped up and she knew he was almost there, she slowed him down until he was calm again. Then, she built the tension again and she continued this way until there was nothing she could do to slow him down. He was so keyed in that the only possible thing left for him to do was to flip her over and fuck her almost to the point of insanity. She moaned and screamed back at him. He held her is a semi choke hold from behind. She gasped as he shuddered with pleasure. Her dripping, creamy vagina was all smiles and sweet aching.

She bit her lip and closed her eyes. She was still feeling the spasm of her orgasm. Her insides collapsed around his still hard dick. He moved in slow motion now, with a beautiful kind of animalistic fervor. They were both covered in delicious sweat. They laid on their backs panting, their fingers barely touching. Sophie could not open her eyes, Max was unable to move. Their breathing and the sunlight were the only audible things in the entire apartment.

Chapter Two

Brenton stood at the back of the room by the bar at Santos Party House. KEV was on stage. The room was packed to the hilt. So many people showed up that they had to turn people away at the door. This was not KEV's regular following. The article in Fader magazine had really opened up his fan base and he was basking in the fanfare. The beat to his newest single was about to drop and he had his head cocked with his hand next to his ear, listening to the entire room sing at the top of their lungs.

> *"We ain't playin'*
> *with these bitches maaaaan-*
> *no no no no nope!*
>
> *We ain't playin'*
> *with these bitches maaaaan-*
> *never, never, never, nope."*

Brenton looked on with a kind of pyric glee. Yes, he was happy that KEV had essentially "made it," but there was nothing socially redeeming about this Ratchet culture he was heading up. When the beat dropped, everything went manic. KEV was like a mechanical bull in a china shop. These innocent white children, regaled in their hipster get-ups, had no way of surviving the wrath of his lyrics.

"Let me see you drop it bitch
Let me see you drop it
Twerk!

Let me see you drop it bitch
Let me see you drop it
Twerk!"

In one fell swoop he had converted a room of mildly cultured New York transplants in search of a small slice of ratchetry, into a room full of ghetto fabulous twerk machines. Everybody was twerking. Twerking like their life depended on it.

That's when Brenton noticed a stylish, slender young woman by the bar who seemed completely unaffected by the insanity she was experiencing. Brenton got that buzz in his blood. He felt it like a religious person feels the Holy Ghost. He already visualized the entire thing in his head. She turned and looked at him as if she heard his thoughts. Brenton nodded in acknowledgement. She smiled then raised her glass of wine to him. The fog-filled room stood still for a split second, he took a deep breath, he raised his rum and coke to her and it was a done deal.

What Brenton did not know was that she was a hunter, and he was her prey. She had come to Santos to find him. Not him specifically, but yes, specifically him. She was not looking for a relationship. She wasn't looking for a someone to bed. She was looking for a good-looking man who would be standing by the bar all by himself.

Brenton was about to head over to her when the bartender placed another rum and coke in front of him.

"Compliments of the lady."

Brenton was shocked, "Really?"

He was impressed. She was good. He smiled to himself. Is this how things look from the other side? By the time he placed his fingers around the glass, she was already flush against him.

"Come with me," she whispered into his ear.

Her voice was filled with the sweet dark elixir of fuck me now. Something inside him clicked. Every muscle in his body was under her spell. He was a lamb and she was a beautiful knife. She had this unexplainable sway over him. He could have said no, he could have stopped to ask her what her name was, but that was not important right now. Her sexual energy was ruthless and all he wanted was what she had to offer; *and Bang*.

Brenton is on his way down the stairs, it was as if he was being carried by some strange ghost of desire. His eyes were glued to her beautiful ass. *I shouldn't be doing this*, he thought to himself. He thought about Emily. He thought about the passion they had. Why was he doing this? Yes, he wanted to let go of this woman's hand but something inside of him would not let him.

"What the fuck is wrong with you Brent," he said in a hushed murmur.

And just when he had made up his mind to turn back, she paused on the devil lit stairs, leaned against the wall, pulled him in slowly, took his hand and slid it up her skirt.

Was her pussy wet? No, it was drenched. It was like a torrential down pour. At this point Brenton knew the vagina gods must have been testing him, and he was more than willing to fail their test. He flipped her around, hiked up her skirt and placed his entire face in her soaking crotch. Her pussy was like an ocean of dripping silk.

A young couple passed them on the stairs. Brenton shot to his feet; *and Bang*.

They are in the women's bathroom and she is sucking centuries, no, eons from his dick. Her tongue was like the bow of a finely tuned violin. She moved up and down the full shaft with a brutal kind of grace. The slurping and kissing sounds had Brenton on his toes in tears.

He was only interrupted by her adlibs, "You love the way I suck it like a whore, don't you? Oh, I am such a dirty little whore."

Brenton was trying his best not to come. He clenched his teeth, tightened his eyes, and before for he could say, *I'm coming*, her mouth was filled with his warm explosion. She moaned and writhed as she swallowed. Brenton was frozen.

She stood up, took his face in her palms, looked him in his eyes and said, "Good boy," as if he was her pet poodle.

Brenton was beside himself.

She kissed him on his cheek, slipped her card into his inside breast pocket, "Call me if you want to play."

She pushed past him to leave the stall.

"What's your name?"

"It's on the card," she did not even look back.

Brenton could not make any sense of what had just happened to him. He pulled the card out of his pocket.

Robyn Merger
VP -Marketing Manager
Morgan Equities

Brenton could still hear the sound of her slurping in his mind. The sweet taste of her juices was still on his lips. He inhaled slowly then headed upstairs.

Chapter Three

"Yow, Brent," Max sounded concerned.

"What's up man," Brenton was barely awake.

It was almost 1pm. He was out all night with KEV. After the show they had gone to about five thousand different spots. Celebrating. They ended the night at Woo Hop in Chinatown.

"You spoke to Maurice lately?"

"Nah, not since your party. What, what's up?"

Max paused and sighed deeply. Brenton knew what was coming next. He thought about Emily, then about Robyn, the girl from Santos Party House, he could still feel her tongue sliding up and down his...

"He found out, right?"

"I'm not sure but I have this feeling that he knows, he has been missing in action since my rooftop party last summer man."

"Why don't you just call Amanda and ask her if he knows?" Brenton was always matter of fact with solutions.

"That's the last person I would want to talk to right now," Max had the sound of failure in his voice, "Can you call Maurice and see what's up with him, you know try to..."

"It's done, I'll call him."

Brenton hung up.

Max hung up, "Fuck!" He felt trapped.

Trapped by not knowing. He ran a million scenarios in his head and in every scenario he ends up murdered by Maurice. He had had so many vivid dreams about being murdered, it took nothing to conjure a horrific scene in his head.

Then it came to him, maybe he should see a therapist. He needed help. He had an affair with his best friend's wife. Maybe he was an addict, or worse a sociopath. Yes- I am a sex addict. If he had a doctor diagnose him he could use that as the excuse. Yeah.

His mind flew to the only time he and Amanda actually had sex in a hotel. All the other times they were in public places. Amanda was the queen of having sex in public.

He recoiled at the thought of him being turned on when Amanda whispered into his ear mid stroke, "Maurice has never fucked me like this, oh my god, you are so deep inside of me."

All Max could think at the moment was, *I shouldn't be doing this*, but something about the entire act turned him on to no avail. His logic was extremely thin, but it was worth a try- Fuck it, it'll work. He imagined himself trying to explain to Maurice that he had been fucking his wife for over a year, because sex addiction.

Chapter Four

Brenton remembered the moment he saw Robyn. His first thought was, *I will fuck you to death*. He had never been more certain of anything. She did this thing to him, she made him into a savage. All the niceties of everyday life were not important to her. She wanted one thing and one thing only. If Emily was a quiet day on the beach in the summer, Robyn was white water rafting. He sent her a text as a feeler, just to say hello.

Brenton: Hi, nice meeting you last night Robyn, this is Brenton

Robyn: I know

Brenton: how would you know, you do not have my number??

Robyn: I told you to text me

Brenton: When, last night?

Robyn: No, just now

Brenton was a little confused.

Brenton: what do you mean?

Robyn: you will understand soon

Brenton: hmmm, how soon?

Robyn: It's Saturday, surprise me. I am at 161 w 15th apt 6D.

And as soon as she hung up, her doorbell rang. It was Brenton. She was in yoga pants and a very thin top. She had the perfect amount of breasts for days.

"Come in, sit down and let me get you something to drink. Maybe you'll get enough strength to tear these off me with your teeth."

Brenton almost died when the words came out of her mouth. She was beyond, she was insane, she was not human.

"What do you do at Morgan Equities?"

"You don't want to know, it's boring stuff."

"I can't imagine you doing anything boring?"

"Really, why is that?"

"Because you, you know, you don't seem like that type of person."

"What type of person?"

She came back into the living area of the loft. The loft was spacious. By the size of the space he knew she had to be making serious bread. She handed him a drink, cranberry and pineapple. He took the glass. She sat on the floor between his legs, looking up at him. He started sweating. It's not that he was nervous, he was not nervous, she just made him sweat. He took a sip as she slowly unbuckled his belt. He was fully erect before she could unzip him.

"What do you want?" She said quietly reaching into his boxers, as if speaking to his dick.

Brenton could not get the words out, he stuttered. She did not hear him. It was as if she was in a zone, she was focused on the task at hand. She licked her lips and took a deep breath. Placed his dick to her nostrils and inhaled.

"Yes," she whispered as she shook her head.

"Wha, what do I want...?" Brenton finally spoke.

She took him into her mouth. He was in dreamland, his eyes rolled back.

"What, what, what do you want from me?"

"I just want you to sit back and enjoy."

And with that she went to work. He reclined into the plush chair and fell off the side of the world into her mouth. A few moments passed, then his phone rang. It was Emily. He wanted to answer but he could not. He was in a fugue state. His phone rang again.

"Answer it, I want to hear the conversation, it totally turns me on," Robyn said with her mouth full.

Brenton's dick got harder.

"What?"

"I know it's your girlfriend, answer it and put it on speaker phone," she smiled and winked at him then slowly licked him from ball to tip.

"Hello?" Brenton answered.

"Hey Brent, how's Robyn?"

Brenton froze, "What?" His heart was in his mouth.

"How is it going?" Emily repeated.

Brenton sighed.

"Ah, ah, I'm good. What are you up to?"

"Just busy, clients, you know. Just wondering if you were free this evening."

"Yeah, no, yeah, I might be... I am."

"Ok, let's do dinner, my place, 8pm. Cool?"

"Yes, that works."

"I'll be wearing something sexy."

"Can't wait to see."

The whole time Brenton was on the phone, Robyn was sucking him slowly and playing with her pussy. And just as he hung up, she let out a primal scream. It was almost as if she was braying. The rawness of her scream motivated Brenton. He grabbed his dick, got on his feet and started working on himself. Her body kept shuddering while she held her mouth open.

"Give it to me, give it to me, give it to me," she got more aggressive with each refrain.

She was in charge in this moment and she knew it. She grabbed his dick just as he was about to come and pumped the entire Permian Basin out of him.

Chapter Five

Daren and Tom are sitting at Mo's waiting for the monthly burlesque show to begin. Once a month on Wednesday's the back room of Mo's is transformed into an improv strip club. Not really a strip club, strip club, but as close as the well-heeled can get to a strip club without feeling guilty about the accompanying misogyny and objectification of women. But hey, hypocrisy is a real thing. Not that anything is wrong with strip clubs or hypocrisy.

The room is squeezed tight with anticipation. There is a mid-thirties older looking white woman with a fraction of the necessary or legal amount of ass required to be on stage, gyrating. She was pale squared, gyrating like she was a spoof of herself. Late-nineties new jack swing has a way of making people look older than they really are. The audience looked on in semi-bewilderment. Her slight pouch and her chicken legs were more than anyone present had paid for.

Daren was sipping a cider trying to look as cosmopolitan as he could, never mind that it was June and he had an ascot and blazer on. Tom had moved up from Cider, he was now a martini man. Since he started working as a real estate agent his whole swag had been updated.

"What does Ms. Thang think she is doing? Ewww...Uhm, someone needs to tell her to get her life."

"She's not that bad, I've seen worst," Tom was trying to soften the blow.

"Worst? Is that even possible? Oh my god, she is scaring these people," Daren's eyes darted around the room, his face scrunched in snobbery, "These people don't know no better. I need to take them to see my girl Right Now Rouge!"

"Is that your friend that tours with-"

"Yes dear, she tours with The Sweet Spot. Chile, they need some of that up in here," a smug air came over Daren as he took a sip from his cider.

He looked up and saw Sheila as she slipped through the thick red curtains, into the back room. Maybe his eyes were playing games with him, but she looked completely different. She had lost about thirty pounds, she had an air of confidence about her that was not there before. He tried his best to make himself invisible but it was virtually impossible to hide a man of his proportions behind a bottle of cider. Tom noticed his uneasiness.

"What's wrong, you seem spooked?"

"Me spooked, nah, no way."

Tom scanned the room to find the source of Daren's unease. Sheila squeezed past a few people as she moved toward the front by the DJ booth where Daren and Tom were sitting.

"Hey Daren," Sheila was beaming.

"Who is that Daren?" Tom was waiting with a side eye and a slight duck mouth, but Daren offered nothing.

"Ahm, just a friend. I met her last summer and she had been a..."

"Gimme hug," Sheila said reaching over the table with her arms and bosoms.

Tom tossed in a sweet, "ok girl," as he tapped her right breast from below.

Daren relented and donated a half hug. His face was clear that he did not want to be at Mo's any more.

"Let me sit next to you."

Tom scooched over, then Daren scooched over as Sheila slid next to him. Her hand found Daren's thigh. Daren froze as a thought flew through the bitter tundra of his head, *what the fuck?* He was breaking into a flop sweat.

Sheila glanced at him sideways with a sneaky smile on her face. She was fully invested in a second episode with Daren. She had been stalking him for almost a full year and she was now at the point of bursting. What she did not know was that Daren was not interested in a repeat episode.

She fingered the waitress, "What are you guys having? My treat."

Daren perked up like a prairie dog, "Ooooh really? I'm having cider," he was so pleased he could hardly contain himself.

"Cider huh? Cider on me all night," she winked.

She was being extremely obvious about what she wanted. Daren gave her the side eye while emptying the cider he had in his hand.

"Martini for me please," Tom's eyes were glued to the disaster of a go-go dancer who was gyrating on stage, her chicken legs were taut with age.

Sheila slid her hand into Daren's lap as she whispered into his ear, "What are you doing after this?"

Daren kindly took her hand out of his lap and placed it on her thigh and whispered in her ear, "I am going home to sleep."

Five ciders later the show was drawing to a close. Daren was slowly beginning to like Sheila more than he should. All those burlesque dancers gyrating on stage must have inspired him. It was not that he wanted to have sex with Sheila per se, he just wanted to be with someone, and he was totally buzzed. And when he gets buzzed, things tend to not matter as much. And Sheila was all giddy next to him, sliding her fingers along his thigh. He could feel a light erection coming on, and before he could think twice about whether he was interested; *and Bang*.

Daren is in the foyer of Maurice and Amanda's home and Sheila is sucking holy Jesus out of his dick. She was like a crazed wolf ravishing a tender doe. And just when he was about to come she stopped, pushed him onto the floor and mounted his dick. No condom mind you. She knew exactly what she was doing. She slid down his anxious erection as he exploded inside of her, moaning all the way down his trembling shaft. Sheila let out a small plea as a jolt of sweetness coursed through her body. And in that moment, she knew it. She could feel it in her bones.

Daren closed his eyes, he was disgusted. *Why the fuck did he do this? Again.*

Chapter Six

"Hey Meghan!" Sophie clasped her arms around Meghan and gave her the tightest hug she had in her arsenal.

"Hey Sophie, long time," Meghan's voice was painted in hesitance.

Meghan missed Sophie but she did not want it to show.

"I know, I know. What have you been up to?"

They pulled apart and looked each other in the eyes.

"Not much, just living. I just feel so blessed, so much has happened since I found the lord."

"The lord?" Sophie pretended that she did not remember, "Wow, yes, yes, yes you did get baptized, right? Girl I thought that was a phase."

Something about Meghan all prim and proper was so sexy to Sophie.

"Yeah, I was surprised too."

"You are the last person I would expect to be dressed like this and...," Sophie paused, she did not want to scare the prey, "and be looking like a conservative snack."

Sophie eyed Meghan up and down. Meghan knew that look and what it meant, but she shook it off.

They were meeting for the first time after a year. So much had happened since. They walked into Peaches, and waited to be seated. The place was a buzz, servers whizzing every which way, bartenders clinking and clanking bottles and glasses. Everything moved like a well-oiled machine doing this abstract gastric dance.

They were seated in the back. They leaned into each other.

"I miss us," Sophie gushed as she touched Meghan's hands across the table.

Meghan took a deep breath, smiled, "I miss us too Sophie."

"So tell me, who is he? Tell me about him. Come on, tell me, tell me."

Sophie got that feeling she used to get when they shared relationship secrets.

Meghan paused. She thought for a while as frame after frame of her relationship with Pastor Emannuel Cox slid through her head. This conservative exterior that she sported was only a camouflage for all the scandalous things she had been up to for the past year. They say you can walk a horse to water but you can never change a woman's sexual appetite.

The past year was a smorgasbord of lovers for Meghan. Yes, she was married to Pastor Emanuel Cox, but there were things about her that she had been hiding from her husband. It was a constant struggle. And lord knows she prayed on it. She had had prayer support from:

- Deacon Matthews
- Senior Pastor Brathwaite
- Jeffery Patterson, the youth fellowship director
- Sister Fabiola Ransom

Fabiola lingered in Meghan's mind for a few seconds.

"He is so amazing, I can't believe how the lord has blessed me with the perfect husband. He is everything I needed in a man."

Meghan showed off her rings.

Sophie was still skeptical. Meghan's prim and proper exterior was for the rest of the world. Sophie knew Meghan, inside and out. Meghan was hiding something.

"Ooh, nice rock," they both laughed.

And for a split-second Sophie saw the old Meghan peek through; *and Bang*.

Sophie and Meghan are in a vicious wrestling match in Sophie's bed. They tore into each other like two old diarists reading fine print. The sexual energy was overbearing. Fuck all the conservative bullshit she was talking about earlier. Fuck all the days and nights she spent in church pretending to love the lord. She was a roaring sexual river and sometimes a river needs to be fed, and bitten, and eaten, and spanked, and splayed, and spread, and kissed, and tongued, and fingered, and fucked, and flipped, and licked, and dominated, and tossed, and choked, and creamed, and studied deeply. You get the fucking point.

Sophie had become extremely proficient at serving up such delights to rivers, especially rivers in need. Meghan screamed her way to a most glorious orgasm.

Sophie smiled with Meghan's sweet juices on her lips. Meghan tasted like prayers.

Meghan was on her back in tears, "Why did we do this? We can't. You know how I feel about you Sophie, why would you...?"

Sophie looked up at her with an evil grin, "Because I can and because you wanted me to."

Chapter Seven

Brenton, Trace, Max and KEV were at The Brooklyn Moon. Mike the owner was behind the bar. It was early evening, and splinters of sunlight trailed into the room, transforming it into a surreal fish bowl filled with wonder. The fish swam around in small whispers flirting with each other.

"So, you're saying you could be in an open relationship?" Max looked at Trace suspiciously as he asked.

"I could," Trace replied with a slight smirk.

"Nah, really?" Max could not believe it.

"Why not? Instead of cheating, why not just keep the lying out of the relationship," Trace said dryly.

"Because no man wants some other man to be pounding out his wife," KEV said with disgust barreling out of his chest.

There was a long pause.

"But your wife is gonna get pounded out either way mate. You might not know it, but someone out there might be laying proper dick to your wife, and guess what, you would never know it man," Trace said without a glimmer of sarcasm.

Max knew exactly what he was talking about because he had done that very thing to another man's wife. He had a few flashes of his escapades with Amanda. The problem he was having was, how does someone broach such a conversation with your significant other?

Brenton was on Trace's side, "I think I could do it. I just wouldn't want to know. She would have to keep that shit to herself."

"Hell fucking nah nigga. Ya'll nigga's are some weak ass mofuckas. How the fuck you go' let your bitch fuck another nigga?" KEV was a thug in full thug bloom, "Get the fuck outta here."

Mike smiled as he watched the verbal sparring. He was mixing up some concoction that was bound to make the conversation better.

"Hold up, before ya'll go any further let me know what you think about this?"

He poured the concoction into shot glasses. They all threw it back.

"That one is called, I will never let another man pound my wife," Mike said jokingly.

They all burst into laughter.

"You new niggas is what's fucking up the game. If you do some shit like that, what is a bitch to do next huh? If she can fuck who ever she wants, what's the point of her being your wife?" KEV was livid.

Trace raised his hand gently in the direction of KEV, "So you're saying that part of her being your wife is that she can only have sex with you right?"

"Yeah, that's what I said," his chest puffed up.

"So can you have sex with other people?" Trace narrowed his eyes as he looked directly into KEV's face.

"But that's different ma nigga," KEV shrugged as he answered.

"Wait a second here, you're saying you can cheat on your wife but for you and your wife to sit down and make it legit would be what?" Trace pretended he was trying to figure out where KEV was coming from.

"I'ma fuck either way, whether she fucking or not, so I don't need to have no fuckin agreement that she can fuck too. What kinda shit is that?" KEV brought the room to a hush.

"That's what the fuck I'm talking about," Max chimed in.

"See that's what's wrong with the world, guys like you who want to do whatever they want, but their women need to stay in their little boxes. You don't think your woman might ever think about another man? Or worse, want to be with another man?" Trace was irritating KEV and he knew it.

KEV looked him dead in his face and spat out, "Well she better keep that shit to herself."

They all chuckled.

"No, but seriously though," Brenton tried to get everyone's attention, "you don't think the same way you get tired of the same old coochie, day in and day out, that your wife or lady or whoever you are with gets tired of having sex with you?"

"Nah, women are different brah."

"How?"

"They ain't like that. Nah, women are cool as long as you take care of home, knowamsayin."

Brenton decided to give the conversation some perspective, "That would make sense if it was the 1800's. But bro, women are no different than men. You ever hear the saying that men are only as faithful as their options?"

"Yes," Mike and KEV replied in unison.

"Well nowadays women have options too, and they are using them."

Chapter Eight

"I don't even know where to start bro," Max was breaking into a flop sweat. "It just happened by accident the first time. I swear to you man, she came on to me, and even when I was trying to tell her to stop, it was as if…," Max was searching for the right word to say.

"Max, we were like brothers bro. Why the fuck would you fuck my wife? Ma fucking wife dude."

Maurice was in pain. Not because he cared that someone was having sex with his wife, no, frankly he did not care either way. He was just in pain because Max was like a brother to him and treachery is harder for him to deal with than infidelity.

"I honestly don't know how to answer that." There was a hundred-year silence.

"I was wrong man. And I am just here trying to set things right," Max's eyes were filled with water.

Maurice studied his face for a while, "Set things right? Set things right? What, you gonna un-fuck my wife? Is that it?"

"Dude, come on man. I didn't mean it like..."

"Get the fuck outta here with that bullshit," Maurice sat back. "As far I'm concerned, you're dead bitch, fucking dead."

"Really? Just like that?"

Max was sad, but deep down he felt like he got away with murder. He was expecting to be killed by Maurice.

"I hope you enjoyed it."

Max looked at Maurice and smiled, and in his mind he said, *yes I fucking enjoyed it*, but he did not mean that.

"You want to know the truth. We hooked up once by accident and the rest of the times I swear she was fucking blackmailing me to keep having sex with her."

"Get the fuck out of here, you really expect me to believe that?"

"I swear on my mother bro," Max said from his soul.

Maurice could see that he was telling the truth. But the truth is sometimes not the thing that fixes things. Maurice looked Max up and down, then reached out his hand. He could feel his entire being shift into corporate mode. In the back of his mind he had devised a plan to destroy Max.

Max took his hand.

"Mm, I believe you man. I believe you," Maurice said with a quiet cunning in his voice and a small smile tucked in the corner of his face.

"Thank you," Max let out a sigh of relief.

The handshake lasted two lifetimes. Maurice gritted his teeth while looking into Max's eyes.

"Does Sophie know that this was going on?" Maurice narrowed his eyes and sliced into Max slowly.

Max panicked in his chest. Maurice noticed his now visible fear. He had Max exactly where he wanted him. Let the games begin he thought to himself.

"You know what, forget it. We've been friends for too long to let pussy get in the way of our friendship. Me and Amanda weren't even dealing like that no way."

Max was nodding; agreeing to agree.

Maurice pulled him in closer, "But that was foul as shit, you know that right?"

"I know man, I don't know what the fuck I was thinking."

"Listen I gotta go get my daughter from her friend's house."

"So we good, right?" Max asked sheepishly.

"We good," Maurice replied assuredly.

Maurice stood up and walked out of The Emerson and into the muggy June night.

Chapter Nine

"Go ahead and sit down," Ms. Clearmont motioned with her hand for Sophie to sit.

Sophie sat, then sat back, then gently crossed her legs and braided her thin fingers into her lap. It was as if she was seeing Ms. Clearmont for the first time.

"So how have you been Sophie?"

"Things have been very good."

"Nice, nice, good to hear."

"Is it?"

Ms. Clearmont sensed a tinge of flirtation in Sophie's tone, so she smiled gently before she answered, "It is always good to hear when my clients are doing well."

"How are things with you?" Sophie uncrossed her legs and leaned forward as she closed her eyes and inhaled.

She could taste hints of Ms. Clearmont flitting around the room, "What's that fragrance?"

"White Diamonds."

"I love that smell," Sophie looked Ms. Clearmont in the eyes as she spoke.

"Tell me, what's going on with you Sophie?"

"Oh, you have no idea the things I have done, I have been doing," Sophie said in her most ravenous voice.

"What have you done Sophie?"

"At first I just wanted to play. You know, just to tease or even flirt with what has been happening inside of me, but it's like sometimes I lose myself in it and…," Sophie drifted off into a day dream.

"Sophie?" Ms. Clearmont was getting turned on by her intensity.

"Yes," she snapped back into Ms. Clearmont's office. "I'm so sorry, that happens to me all the time now."

"What happens all the time now?"

"I just drift off and all I think about when I do is sex. I just get flashes of sex I have had, or I imagine myself…," Sophie paused as if for effect.

Ms. Clearmont leaned in, "Go ahead."

"I sometimes imagine myself getting fucked," she paused again, "by a total stranger in a public place," she exhaled.

Ms. Clearmont started jotting down notes franticly, "And when did this start?"

"I don't know, maybe a month or two ago? It kind of crept up on me, you know, like one day I was normal and the next day all I could think about was sex, sex, sex, sex. All day all night. Is that normal?"

"Well normal is a loaded word," Ms. Clearmont kept her head in her notes.

She was trying her hardest not to engage Sophie on the level she was looking for.

"I think I might be a sex addict. Is that bad? I literally want sex all the time."

"There we go again. It's not about bad or good, it's about the way this, quote, addiction affects your everyday life. By the way, what made you say sex addict instead of any other thing?"

Sophie crossed her legs and eased onto her left butt cheek. She was doing kegel exercises. She loved the sensation as the muscles inside her vagina clenched. In her mind she was imagining Ms. Clearmont on her knees in front of her with her entire face in her lap, just licking and slurping. And just like that she closed her eyes and threw her head back as a beautiful orgasm tore through her body.

Ms. Clearmont saw it all happen.

"So, Sophie have you tried to control your sexual behavior?"

"Control? This is the most I have ever been connected to my sexuality, why would I want to control it?"

"So why are you telling me about it?"

"Well, I just, I just need someone I can talk to about it, about the things I have been doing, the things I have been feeling."

"What have you been doing?" Ms. Clearmont stopped being a therapist for a second, she wanted all the juicy details.

Sophie sensed her delight and poured out story, after story, after story, after story...,"and then I slowly pulled his face into my lap and he ate my pussy so, so, so good."

Ms. Clearmont tried her best to maintain her composure, "So, how does that work with your engagement?"

"I'm still engaged," Sophie said as if she did not make the connection between her sex-ploits and her engagement.

Ms. Clearmont was quiet for a few beats, just mulling over what Sophie had said. In the meantime, Sophie was working on her third serving of kegel induced orgasm.

"Do you still have sex with your fiancé?"

A sly smile bloomed on Sophie's face, "All the time, our sex life is all the things and then some, only issue is," Sophie paused and thought about what she was about to say.

"There's an issue?" Ms. Clearmont leaned in

"I haven't had sex with him as myself in months. We mostly have roleplay sex, which is fine, it's just that."

"Just that what?" Ms. Clearmont was on the edge of her chair.

"Nothing," Sophie said innocently.

Ms. Clearmont noted her response then continued writing furiously in her note book, she paused for a second, then jumped to her feet and hurried over to the back of the room. She searched through a few books, riffling through them like a money counter. In that moment of solitude Sophie was taking a deep breath and exhaling very gently.

"I think I know what's happening to you, and this is extremely uncommon," she looked at Sophie as if she were a rare bird. "Not only are you a sex addict, you have a condition called sexual anorexia."

Chapter Ten

Daren was a ball of nervous energy. He was stressed because he was no good at breaking hearts. He could not sit still for a micro second, his brain was tightening in his skull. He looked at his phone, it was 9:59 pm. He was waiting for Sheila to show up. In the back of this mind he was hoping she would not show. Why the fuck was he even doing this. Last week was a mistake. The first time was a mistake. After her text message today, he knew he had to tell her the truth.

At 10 pm on the dot, Sheila strolls through the door in a red dress to murder the entire room. Her dress said, *this is my new body. Yes, I am sexy as hell and I am here to fuck. Thank you.*

Daren was impressed by the dress. He ambled over uncomfortably and met her by the door. They walked over to the bar.

"Cider, right?"

"No, I'm drinking martinis tonight."

"Look at you on your grown man shit."

"Whatever, I *been* on my grown man shit."

"I hear that... alright," she said flirtatiously.

Sheila ordered drinks for both of them. They sat by a cluster of tables close to the bathroom. The conversation was dry until the third drink and Daren decided to get into the reason why they needed to talk. Sheila was prepared for him to tell her that he did not want to see her anymore, hence the dress. The right dress at the right time can be a game changer. She was convinced her dress had changed his mind.

"So, I wanted to see you because," and just then Daren tried his best to feign sincerity, "me and you will not work out."

"Daren, I know that."

"You do?"

"Yes, I do."

"Then, what was last week?"

"Last week, last week, it was nothing."

"Nothing?"

"Daren, I just wanted to fuck that's all. We don't have to go together to do that, right?"

Daren was confused, here he was thinking that she was caught up with him, when in fact she was... Something moved inside of Daren that he had never felt before. He felt thoroughly rejected. It was painful. He tried to get up to go to the bathroom. The Martinis said, *sit down*.

Sheila waved over a well-dressed young man who had been sitting at the bar staring at her. He sat at the table with both of them.

"Hi, how are you, my name is Philip, everybody calls me H."

"Hi, I'm Sheila and this is my friend Daren."

"What's up?" Daren was not happy about this set up.

His heart was breaking in his chest and now he had to deal with this dude.

"So, what's going on?" Philip said in Sheila's direction as if he wanted her to leave with him.

"He just broke up with me, if you can call it that," Sheila was trying to make Daren jealous.

"No I didn't," Daren spat out.

"This Dude? Dumped you? What? So why you still here with him?

Sheila looked at Philip with his chiseled features and muscular arms, then she looked at

Daren and kissed her teeth. Daren's mouth fell open; *and Bang*.

Sheila is in the backseat of a min-van with one leg on the roof and the other braced against the baby seat in middle row, with Philip ten fathoms deep inside her. He was moving like a man possessed. He went so deep, she kicked the baby seat out of its buckle.

Daren sat inside Casablanca and nursed his martini for the next half hour while Sheila had her pussy stroked and eaten in every possible language. She did not even get Philip's number. She knew that a man like that was no good for her.

She walked like an injured athlete back into Casablanca to find Daren slumped over in the corner. A sad feeling came over her. She went over to him and asked to help him get home.

"I'm good," Daren slurred, pushing her away.

"No you're not, let me get you an Uber home."

"I'm good. I'm good."

Sheila took out her phone and called an Uber pool.

The Uber pulls up outside of Maurice and Amanda's house.

"Wanna come in?" Daren said wobbling.

"No. We're done, right?"

"Yeah, yeah, I forgot."

"Well, see you around," she gestured towards the door.

Daren reached in for a kiss.

Sheila caught his face, looked him in his eyes then gently asked, "You sure 'bout this?"

Daren answered, "Yes, I'm sure."

They kiss gently. Daren paused for a moment. If he was not drunk, he would say her lips tasted like... Dick?

Chapter Eleven

Amanda stepped into the brilliance of the Brooklyn Saturday afternoon like a woman out to conquer kingdoms. The newly converted Brooklynites were brunching like so many cosmopolitan wildebeest. She hated New Brooklyn with a passion. She despised all the new transplants who swore up and down about the dangers of gentrification. She hated how they harken back to the golden years before Brooklyn lost all its swag. All the way back to three years ago when they did not have to wait on a list to get brunch. Whenever she heard them yapping all nostalgic, she would roll her eyes so hard she would get a migraine. In her mind, she tried her best not to scream, *Bitch, I been here my entire life, three years?! Three years ain't shit!*

But gentrifiers aside, it was a beautiful day in Brooklyn. It was as if the trees were being paid to be the perfect shade of green. It was as if everyone in the streets were cast by some Hollywood agency. The scene on any given day in this area of Brooklyn was something like a cross between Afro-punk and Coachella. It was as if the cars moving down the boulevard were synchronized with the tweeting birds in the trees.

The huddle of new stores that had popped up on Myrlte Ave in the last week or so had that look of optimistic doom.

Yes, your pop-up fashion house is sleek and sexy and postmodern and has all the trappings of Chelsea, but this is Brooklyn, in a month you will be closed.

Yes, your art bar that only serves shark blood mojitos and squid ink gourmet pizza is cute, but nobody in Brooklyn wants that shit. You will be out of business in an hour.

She walked down Myrtle Ave throwing her ass like a funeral procession, looking into the store fronts wondering, *where are these people getting money for these useless ideas.* She saw a lonely waiter in the shark blood mojito bar and thought about Max; *and Bang*.

She is sitting in Max's lap in room 809 of Aloft Brooklyn. Their eyes were tied together as he stroked upward into her quietly and slowly. She felt him in every part of her existence. She gyrated slowly as they locked lips. He grasped both cheeks of her ass, opened her wider so he could get in deeper. She literally felt like he hit her heart.

A cold chill came over her body as he slid gently out of her, then back in with passion. She looked up at the ceiling and in that moment, she knew she had fallen in love with Max. Something inside of her wanted to hate him. Fuck him. He was just supposed to be a revenge fuck. But here she was getting all up in her feelings. And just when she was about to shed a silent tear, he flipped her over and went in even deeper.

She felt him in her liver. In her chin. In her fingers. And maybe it was the light from the Manhattan skyline, or maybe it was the ocean trapped in the sheets, or maybe it was just all the memories of all the love she had never gotten from Maurice, but she just broke out into a fit of tears. She was bawling. She was having an orgasm and a mental breakdown - or

a mental breakthrough - at the same time.
Whatever it was, it was new, it was different.
She had never felt this feeling before.

Chapter Twelve

Max was kicking himself, *fuck - fuck.* Why was he back here, again?

He lay on his back looking up at the ceiling. He could hear Amanda sobbing.

"You, ok?" He asked her quietly.

"Yeah, yea...I'm fine," the words were coated in tears.

He reached over and touched her hesitantly. His touch made her cry harder. Max did not know what to make of it, but for some reason her crying aroused him. He was ashamed to feel what he was feeling, but his dick could not deny the sexual motivation he got from watching her sobbing into the sheets. Now he was at a crossroads. How does he comfort her when touching her makes her cry harder? Also, how do they have sex again without him touching her?

He had to figure something out. This was a battle brewing in his head and body. He should just leave and pretend nothing happened. Nothing happened. Nothing happened. He would never respond to another text from her.

He stood up to get dressed. Moving as slowly as he could, he gathered up his clothing. His dick was in no mood to leave.

Amanda rolled over from her sobbing. It was as if Max was invisible. All she saw was his dick, vein-filled and floating in the room like Banquo's ghost. She reached out her left hand. For a second, Max tried to refuse, but then she pouted and he knew he had to do what had to be done.

His dick gave him a high five as they both slid all the way into Amanda's warm insides. Not caring about the consequences, she tore the condom off of his dick and for the first time he physically felt her velvety pleasure; felt the aching wretchedness of her gyration; felt her creamy corridors grasping tightly against his durable dick.

He passed out and came back to life every time he entered her. Each time he went in was the first time. Her pussy was like Groundhogday, it was a sunrise and a sunset made out of slippery flesh.

After fifteen steady minutes of beautiful surrender, of the slapping sounds of flesh on flesh, of tongue and mouth and hips and teeth and fingernails and moans and slow, slow penetration, she felt his orgasm building. And just when he was about to explode, she slid out from under him and took him into her mouth all the way to his balls. Max was amazed. She gagged as he ejaculated a wonderful sermon into her mouth. She licked her lips quietly, looked up at him, then smiled glassy-eyed and glowing.

Max felt like something was different about her. What it was, he did not know. But something was different.

Chapter Thirteen

Max was lost. He just kept thinking, *Why did you do that Max?* What he did made no sense. He had just cleared up the insanity of this whole thing with Maurice and here he was right back in the fire, AGAIN. He sat back in the Uber with a sad pained expression on his face. He had disappointed himself. He was an animal. He had done this thing without any real pressure. He had done it for the thrill. He could not say Amanda was forcing him anymore. He wanted to know why. He had to find out why he was such a fucking animal.

He pulled up in front of his building. Sophie was waiting for him. She had on a beautiful summer evening dress. She slid into the Uber next to him and kissed him on the cheek.

"How was your day babe?"

"I hate working Saturdays," Max said in his best faux-sad voice. He felt like a whore.

"How was your day?" He asked with a slight yawn.

Sophie had a quick flash of herself standing with her legs obliquely spread, her ass gently indented by the edge of the desk as Ms. Clearmont poured a bottle of Malbec over her breasts and licked her nipples slowly as the maroon liquid meandered down her toned core. Sophie's imagination was like a movie studio, pumping out scenes, situations and episodes to keep her appetite at bay.

"Had an amazing session at the therapist's," Sophie said with a sly smile. "I had a major breakthrough today."

Sophie had a quick flash of Ms. Clearmont's face planted perfectly into her crotch. She squeezed her pelvic floor as she imagined Ms. Clearmont's nose tenderly grazing her clit. Sophie licked her lips and closed her eyes for a second, and just like that she had a tiny explosion and her lap became juicier.

Max felt her sexual energy, "Are you ok?" He said looking at her sideways with a smile.

"Yes, I am, I'm perfect," she eyed Max sideways.

Max knew that look. She took his hand and slid it down her thighs all the while thinking about Ms. Clearmont's. The lips of her vagina whispering wetness. He lightly passed his finger print across her trembling clit while looking directly into her eyes. She took a deep breath as the ghost of his finger haunted her juicy vagina. She slid down into the seat. She wanted him to slip a finger in but he would never do such a thing. Instead, he scooped some of her juices onto his middle finger and placed it in his mouth. She felt herself coming. She closed her eyes and eased into it. Max smiled.

"We should stop here, let's turn around and go home," Sophie whispered filled with yearning.

"But we have to go meet Brenton and Emily at Lunatico."

Max wanted to go out, he had had a crazy day. He needed a drink and some music, something to get his mind off of the insanity that was about to destroy his life.

Sophie was reeling inside. She wanted Max inside her, she gyrated slowly in her seat.

"But when we get home you're in trouble mister," Sophie whispered into Max's ear.

Max laughed as she sucked on his finger.

Chapter Fourteen

Young Kevlar sat in the gospel of weed smoke like the messiah during the transfiguration. The extremely small green room of Santos Party House was stuffed to the gizzards with a congregation of fiending fans. KEV had done shows and had had fans who wanted to take pictures backstage, but this was a new experience for him. These people were fanatic, they weren't just fans. He could actually taste the fame in his palms. They wanted him. They would do anything to be next to him, to be close to him. It was strange and he loved it.

Marla, who was now his assistant toggled her way through the smoke and whispered in KEV's ear. KEV pointed at three young women waiting by the back wall. With that, Marla nodded at the security and in one boisterous shout he had the attention of the entire room.

"Everyone that way."

His flashlight above his head, "Ok let's go, let's go."

His almost seven-foot frame spoke louder than his voice.

The room was clear in the blink of an eye. Marla looked at the ladies, all duck-mouthed and knock-off designer chic, and rolled her eyes.

"I'll be back in fifteen minutes," she said in a half snark.

As she exited the room the ladies jumped on KEV like a thirsty clutch of vampires. They went straight for his zipper and did things to him he could have never imagined. KEV did not know it was possible to get a blow job from three women at the same time. They passed his dick from mouth to mouth without using their hands. All the while kissing each other and moaning, fingering themselves, and tasting each other, and kissing him, and spitting on his dick, and talking to it like it had done something wrong.

He grabbed on to the sides of the couch as if he was in a rocket taking off to the sweetest heaven. He felt every micron and muscle of his body stand at attention. And just when he was about to ejaculate, he felt one of the young lady's tongue slide carefully into his ass. The entire universe receded, and his life stopped. He moaned like a cat in heat being strangled and drowned, as he shot his semen across the room like a supersonic jet breaking the sound barrier. Young Kevlar saw stars. When he opened his eyes, he was a new man.

Chapter Fifteen

It was euphoric inside of Lunatico. The mood was syrupy, the music was dripping in all things sexy. A dirty sexual dirge was locked away at the back of the room by the audience. The sound slipped between, around, and through their softly perspiring bodies.

Lunatico feels like a juke joint in the middle of an African village, except that that African village has mixologists who make delightful drinks that taste like abstract art. After a few minutes the facade wears on you and you realize the African village had been colonized, and that it is not really a village but a resort town somewhere near Naples Florida in a retirement home. It's not that the place is fake or pretentious, it's more that it tries too hard to be itself.

On stage stirring up an enormous pot of musical stew was a musician all dressed in white, with the most perfect shade of black skin imaginable. He was a man made from the most flawless onyx, his porcelain teeth like a beautiful jackal. He was in another world as he played.

Sophie had her eyes closed the entire time. And all through the performance she was imaging the sable hands of this stranger giving her a full body massage, plucking her strings the way he was plucking that instrument. Every note he hit, hit something inside of her. She started making plans of who she would be for Max when she got home. Maybe she'll be this stranger's wife, lost in Brooklyn looking for a place to stay for the night.

After the music Brenton and Emily went to the bar.

Sophie whispered in Max's ear, "I don't think I can wait until we get home."

Max was turned on by the very idea. Sophie had developed an appetite for sex that was thrilling to Max.

She took his hand and led him to the back garden. He sat on a chair and she sat side saddle on his lap. Her flowing floral dress draped over his pelvis. And in a subtle choreographed move Max unzipped his pants, her dress flaring up then falling in slow motion, as he gently slid her panties to the side and slid into her eager pussy. Her body shook upon entry.

Sophie pretends to whisper something into his ear. Max pretends to laugh. Sophie pretends to laugh. The other patrons are totally unaware of the fact that Max's dick is choked to the hilt inside of Sophie. Her juices sliding down the shaft of his dick and into his lap. She rocks back and forth and throws her head to the side and laughs so that she can grasp him tighter. She falls forward to get extra friction from his slow exit then slowly settles all the way down onto his dick as he thrusts upward. They sit and talk and laugh for fifteen solid minutes, slowly edging orgasms out of each other. Sophie pointed at the stars, Max followed suit as they both came.

Brenton and Emily came into the back-garden double-fisting drinks.

"For you Sophie," Emily handed Sophie a glass of Cabernet.

Brenton handed Max a rum and coke. They sat and laughed and talked late into the night.

The sounds of the summer walking about in the distance was beautiful.

Chapter Sixteen

"Yow."

"Sup."

"What's good."

"Nothing much, just here."

"You heard about Trace's birthday party?"

"What? Why would I not? That's my cousin, you know that right?"

"I know, I know," Max said drily. "Let's grab a drink by Casablanca before we go."

"What time is good?" Brenton wanted to catch up with his boy. "Nine?"

"Damn, that's too late. I wanted to catch up, lots of crazy shit been happening man."

"Ok, how about seven. I can meet you straight after work."

"I leave work at five bro, seven is not straight after work."

"Ok, ok, it's just that I have a ton of work to get done. I just took on a new artist and KEV is blowing the fuck up man."

"How's that going?"

"It ain't even making no sense bro, he went from like two shows a month to ten offers per day," Brenton sounded overwhelmed.

"Looks like you're gonna need a lawyer soon," Max said laughing.

"Shoot, I need me one of them Manhattan lawyers now."

"Let's talk about it," Max said plotting.

Maybe he could hitch his wagon to Brenton's star. He loved the law, but he hated prosecuting young black men for petty crimes and destroying their lives.

"We could do that," Brenton said pensively, thinking about getting someone else in this sad, sad business of Trap music.

Brenton loved the music business but he did not like the content of what KEV was saying lately. Fortunately, he loved the trappings of the life he was living, so he did it because people wanted it. If left to his own devices he would rather represent an artist like Talib Kweli.

"So, see you at six?" Max said in a higher than normal pitch.

"Fuck it, see you at six," Brenton gave in.

Chapter Seventeen

Friday evenings in Brooklyn come with a sound track and backup dancers. Shit, it comes with extras and a two-thousand-piece orchestra playing all the moods that have ever existed since the first bit of cosmic slop crawled out of the water a few billion years ago.

The craziness in the evening air was tangible. Everybody was somebody and nobody at the same time. That woman with the afro the size of the Sahara was the last surviving member of a royal house in the Sudan. The gentleman all dressed in black at the bar wearing a bowler hat is a time traveler who is in Brooklyn from the year 1849. The dog sitting by the door of the bakery walked out of an oil painting that's on display at the Museum of Modern Art. That little baby crying in the stroller is from a future place and time.

Brooklyn was crowded with old and new feelings, with beautiful moods and melancholy memories.

On Fridays Brooklyn is a hot fuck in a side alley, on a sad back porch, on a fire escape, or some unimportant place dipped in a juicy kind of hunger. Brooklyn on Fridays is a study in flawed perfection. All the broke rich kids come here from every place in the world. Every dreaming artist comes here to become the next Basquiat or the next Jay Z. Some of these kids sadly will never make it, but it is beautiful watching them try.

Trace walked into the Brooklyn Moon, to a round of applause. His newly minted friends that he had borrowed from his cousin Brenton were all there. It was easy being trace. What was there not to love. He was always in a suit. He had an English accent and enough charm to talk a siren onto a ship.

The night air was flavored with all the good things. The room was packed to a level of sexual suffocation that only makes sense in New York, packed enough that you may fear dying but you don't want to miss out on this death. Yeah, it was that packed.

There were beautiful people of all the visible spectrums. And they were all there for one of a million things. They came to party, to slay, to throw it back, to turn it loose, to scream, or shake, or flirt, or pull, or whisper into something, or be whispered into. They came for many things but mostly they came for the highlight reel.

The highlight reels are the brunch stories. And what is a Saturday in Brooklyn without brunch and the decadent indulgences from the night before. Nothing. So, they threw drinks back, they laughed, they whispered, maybe a little dance here, a little flirty flirt there. It was all good and it was all done with impeccable swag.

The chaos was at an orgasmic crossroads when everything froze. Trace had a shot of vodka held high above his head. Brenton was hanging on to him, egging him on. Max was looking on. The owner Mike was pouring another round. Trace's date held onto his other hand. The entire room was in a bacchanalian upheaval that was so unusual in *New Brooklyn* it felt criminal. It was a photo snapped one second before Armageddon.

In this state of exacted bliss, in walks Vanessa. Trace literally swallowed her with his shot of vodka.

"Hey Brent, who is that?" He made a face as if to say, *what the fuck*.

Brenton looked at the door, saw Vanessa and replied, "god."

"I fink you might be right mate," Trace was plotting.

His date for the night pulled him closer. He had already forgotten about her.

Just as Trace was about to move in Vanessa's direction, she smiled and pointed in his direction and screamed, "Max!"

Max did not know what to do. Sophie was right next to him, and Vanessa had always been a contentious issue in their relationship.

"Hey, how are you?" Max avoided her name.

She looked him up and down flirtatiously. And in that moment Sophie knew it. Vanessa had just eye-fucked her man. Trace and Brenton saw the entire episode. Trace's mouth was still agape. Sophie looked Vanessa up and down and smiled. Vanessa smiled back. Sophie reached out her hand, Vanessa took it, and in that very intimate moment they had a truce.

Sophie pulled Max to the side, still holding onto Vanessa's hand, and gently whispered into his ear, "You didn't tell me Vanessa was gonna be here?"

Max did not know what to say. He broke out into a flop sweat and a fit of stuttering, "I. I. I. I. I. I..."

"She's cute," Sophie whispered while looking at Vanessa.

Vanessa saw the look of uncontrollable desire in Sophie's eyes. Sophie wanted something, and she wanted it really bad. Vanessa angled her head like a rare bird and smiled flirtatiously. And once again the entire room stopped, and for a moment only Sophie and Vanessa existed.

In that blip of time, an entire lifetime slipped through both of their heads and bodies. They had one shared feeling.

"I have to talk to you in private," Sophie pulled Vanessa's hand into her body as she whispered.

The room moved as Sophie and Vanessa made their way toward the bathroom in the back of the room; *and Bang*.

Chapter Eighteen

"**W**ho the fuck was that mate?" Trace demanded.

"I. She. I. She. I. I," Max was still stuck in his stutter.

"She is fucking amazing bruv, you gotta introduce me."

"What about your date?"

"My date. Fuck my date. I'm going to marry that woman."

"What? You don't even fucking know her."

"I don't have to know her bruv."

"I guess somethings don't change."

"What does that mean? Listen, you have to live man. I go at life as hard as I can," the alcohol was swilling around in Trace's head, "and if there's one thing I know, that woman is gonna be my wife."

Sophie and Vanessa were standing in the bathroom leaned up against opposite walls looking at each other, trying to figure out what was this thing they were feeling.

"I know what happened, between you and Max last year."

"Really? What happened?" Vanessa was defiant in her tone.

Sophie pressed into the wall, licked her lips, crossed her arms and whispered rockstarly, "I know ya'll fucked."

She was aroused by her own daring.

Vanessa smiled and thought for a long while.

"How do you know that?"

"I can smell you, those natural oils are very distinct. I've been haunted by your smell for the longest," Sophie had a stern look in her eyes.

She was looking for Vanessa's tell. This was a bathroom stand-off like no other. Vanessa's lip jumped. Sophie pounced, "I fucking knew it."

"I, well we didn't. I'm sorry, but we never," Vanessa was falling over her words.

"You don't have to lie," Sophie said feeling like a boss when the words came out of her mouth.

"I'm not," Vanessa paused for a few seconds, "you know what?" She seemed to change gears.

"I'm sorry you had to find out like this. I never meant for this to happen," she felt like she had let down her fellow woman.

And in one swift movement, Sophie was flushed against Vanessa's body with a fist full of her hair clenched and dragged to the side. Sophie felt a warm excitement coursing through her body. Vanessa's mouth was open as she fought against the pain. The pain was sexy. She wanted to fight back but something inside of her said no. She shivered slowly, as Sophie whispered into her mouth.

"I should fucking snap your neck. There ain't no short cuts in life bitch. If you ever wanna fuck my man, I suggest you consult with me first."

Vanessa did not know what to do, what to think, or how to feel. Only one thing was certain, her panties were soaking wet.

Sophie let go of her hair then stood in front of Vanessa like an old nun, and said in her best fake English accent, "There, that's sorted."

She smiled as she straightened out both their clothes.

Vanessa, in some strange way, had surrendered completely to Sophie.

"We should definitely stay in touch. Let's hang out some time," Sophie whispered dryly has she tapped Vanessa on the nose with her index finger.

"We should? We should, we should," Vanessa said, her body still tingling with sexual fright.

Sophie took Vanessa's phone from her hand and typed her number into the phone.

"Call me later tonight, let's go dancing."

Sophie then handed the phone back and smiled.

Vanessa took her phone back. Sophie traipsed off. All Vanessa could think was, *What the fuck just happened?*

Chapter Nineteen

Sophie slid under Max's arm and hugged him. Max was expecting the worst. He knew in the back of his mind that their relationship was over. He knew they could have only talked about one thing. Did he have sex with Vanessa.

"She told me everything," Sophie said looking up at Max with a torturing smile.

She pinched him in the side. Max looked off into the distance.

The truth was, Sophie did not care either way. This was all a game for her now. She wanted Vanessa even more than Max wanted her.

"It doesn't have to be all sneaky Max," Sophie whispered in his ear.

Trace was introducing himself to Vanessa. She was numb to everything he was saying. His mouth was moving, but there were no words.

"I swear to you Sophie, it's not what you think it is."

"Max, don't say anything. I already know, you don't have to belittle her. Look at her, she's sexy, she's beautiful, I can see why you're attracted to her."

"I, but I am not attracted to her like that."

"Max fucking stop!"

And just like that, everyone went silent. The music literally stopped, and their entire business was naked on the bar of the Brooklyn Moon.

Sophie grabbed Max's hand and pulled him outside onto the sidewalk. The new locals were milling by like evening traffic.

"I don't think you're understanding me Max."

"What am I missing?"

"I think we can figure out another way."

"Another way?"

"Yes Max, another way."

Max intuitively knew what she meant but he was being extremely cautious. He knew he was already in deep shit, so he was not trying to take any risks.

"What does that mean though."

"We should talk about being open, about being honest. A year or two ago this would have been an insane idea, but I'm beginning to think that old Sophie was a stupid little child who believed in Santa Clause."

"Open? Open like see other people?"

"No, not open like see other people," Sophie said drily.

"Then what are you talking about?"

"Open like, if you have any desires we can talk about them and we can figure out ways to make them happen."

"But what about you?"

"Well, open goes both ways."

Max paused, he thought about another man being with Sophie. Something inside the flesh of his head hated the idea, but he saw how much she was willing to give him so that he could be a better person. He wanted to do the same for her. But the fact of a thing is always more brutal than the myth of a thing.

Chapter Twenty

KEV and his entourage passed Sophie and Max at the door. They exchanged pleasantries with all those who were deserving. KEV stood by the crowded bar and scanned the room like a hawk looking for prey. He was looking for Daren. And perched atop a tiny bench in the corner, beneath the two framed paintings by Kehinde Wiley, was Daren like a Cheshire cat in royal regalia. His legs awkwardly crossed for one reason and one reason only, to show off his fancy socks. Fancy socks, that was his new thing.

KEV shouted to Mike behind the bar, "A round of shots for the entire bar on me."

It was a gesture mostly toward Daren, but he had to operate in secret. The moment he said it, Daren knew exactly what KEV had intended.

Everyone in the bar cheered. One of Brooklyn's own had made it and had made good on his promise to not forget the little people. The cheers motivated KEV in a delightful kind of way, so he shouted to Mike again.

"Fuck it, make that two rounds Mike."

The bar exploded again. There was so much merriment in that little room, it could have been bottled and sold as seasoning. It could have been bottled and use to feed starving children. It could have been used to fuel a trip to mars.

The night moved, and the little speaker in the corner pumped one perfect song after another. And somewhere between 10:30 pm and the end of the world, the trademark grit of one of New York's most loved staccato beats jumped out the speakers.

"Yeah, yeah,
Am up at Brooklyn.
Now am down in Tribeca,
Right next to DeNiro."

The entire bar joined in like a street savvy gospel choir with something to prove. They sang until their lungs were chafed. They sang as if they were dying. Their voices from different walks of life, from different pieces of the planet, but when the chorus kicked in they knew they were in the greatest city on earth.

"In New York
Concrete jungle
where dreams are made of
there nothing you can't do
I love New York."

Trace was at peak happiness. His English hands in the air, shouting at the top of his lungs. And it was that moment that he knew he was officially over London. Fuck London. He was in Brooklyn with the coolest people ever. They sang like lovers and friends, sang until the night air wept. And the turmoil of the night and the alcohol spilled over into their zewekies.

Chapter Twenty-One

"**W**here to next?" Trace asked as if he was bored of the Brooklyn Moon.

"Let's go to The Back Room," Brenton replied as if he was waiting for Trace to ask.

"How's this gonna work?"

"Uber, one sec let me get a count."

Brenton gawked around The Brooklyn Moon haphazardly in his half-drunken state. It was like counting crazy people in an insane asylum. No one would stand still.

"Hey, hey everybody," he screamed at the top of his voice, "I'm trying to get a head count of who wants to go to The Back Room."

For a second he had their attention, but he knew it would not last.

"If you wanna roll, please wait outside with Trace."

A platoon of half-lit partiers spilled out the bar and onto the side walk like a small stampede. They droned about in the night air, like blips on a radar map. Brenton took a count, then got Max, Sophie and Trace to order Ubers.

The Ubers arrived like serial killers. A few minutes later they were jetting across the Manhattan bridge towards the Lower East Side. The night felt special. Trace was squeezed between his female friend and Daren in the back of one UBER. KEV followed the Ubers in his blacked-out SUV. His entourage was his driver, who almost never speaks, and six women, each one a specific act of god.

KEV had no qualms about exploiting the privileges of his newly expanded fame. He had struggled for too long to not bask in the fruits of his labor. His phone rang. It was Daren.

"Thanks for ignoring me."

KEV cupped the phone to his ear and whispered quietly, "What the fuck man? I told you about this shit."

"What shit?"

"About fucking calling me like this."

"Calling you like what?"

KEV scanned the face of all the women in the SUV as he broke out into a flop sweat, "Calling me in public."

"Calling you in...," Daren paused for a second, "calling you in public? I don't have to call you at all, Ok."

"No, no, no, I was just saying it would be better if you texted me. Can you text me instead?"

KEV was desperate to see Daren alone, so he was in no real place to dictate the parameters of their communications.

Daren rolled his eyes, "Ok, whatever. I will text you then. I just can't take all this secret shit you be on."

KEV was quiet for a few seconds. He took a deep breath, "Just text me."

"Alright, alright," Daren sighed into the phone; *and Bang*.

Chapter Twenty-Two

The Back Room is in the Lower East Side. It would be impossible for you to find the location if you were not told specifically where to look. The entrance is down some stairs and through a narrow, barely lit alley, then through a metal gate, then up a flight of stairs. The path feels like the route to a 90s crack house, but when you push the entry door open it is as if you stepped through a time portal into the year 1925.

Brenton had planned this portion of the evening's festivities because Trace loved this kind of vibe. Trace's date for the evening was upset that he had spent the entire trip to The Back Room talking to Vanessa.

"I'm not gonna sit here and watch you flirt with this woman all night," she was livid.

"How about this love, how about we get you a cab and send you home, it's my birthday. I'm just talking to someone that came to my party. What do you think is gonna happen? Do you think I'm gonna run off with her?"

"No, but, but you are here with me. I want to be here, but you gotta want me to be here too."

"Listen Victoria, I want you to be here. I want us to have a good time, but you can't be up under me every second of every moment. Look around, there are a million people here. Go mingle."

Victoria pursed her lips and made a sad face. Trace took her hand and led her to the small dance area between the couches, and they danced like an old couple with no care in the world.

The salsa transported them to Havana, Cuba. The night was humid and sticky with lust and all the other carnal things that floated off the heads of the drums. The gold-tinged air was perfumed with the grand rituals callused onto the fingers of the drummers. Every cowbell was a novel written about lost love, every movement of her body pulled him back and forth through time, back and forth through the memories of different times and places.

Victoria was a professional dancer. In her arms Trace was a beautiful instrument. The entire party of friends stopped to watch them dance. As the song came to a climactic end, Trace started dragging folks to their feet to join in the dancing. The sexy spirit of salsa snaked into their bodies, and for a moment all their movements were perfect.

Daren was dancing with Vanessa. Sophie was dancing with Trace. Max was dancing with Emily. Brenton was dancing with Victoria. KEV sat in the mouth of the deep red velvet couch draped in women, smiling like a child.

The music switched and everyone exchanged partners. Trace was back to dancing with Victoria. Max was now dancing with Sophie. And maybe it was the music or maybe it was the dim lights, or the alcohol, or the wooden floors, or the tea cups doubling as wine glasses, or the copper mugs filled with Moscow mules, but the couples all started making out as couples.

Daren did not know what to do. He was in the arms of Vanessa. She was beautiful and sexy with a thin layer of sweet on her cheeks, but he was more interested in someone else.

Sophie pulled Vanessa into her and Max's kiss. Max's entire world went dark. He knew for sure he was dreaming, but this felt really real. *Am I dreaming?* He thought to himself.

"I wanna watch you fuck her Max," Sophie whispered into Max's ear in the most sadistic voice Max had ever heard from her.

With that statement, Max knew for sure that it was a dream. But it felt so real. It felt so real he could taste the red wine on Vanessa's lips. He could feel Sophie's nails sinking into his back; *and Bang*.

They are in the back of an Uber making out. Everything blurred. They are on the elevator going up to the apartment. And for a split-second Max was totally sober, and he was struck with panic. Sophie walked out of the elevator holding Vanessa's hand. It was as if Vanessa was her little pet. Max shoved his key into the door. He looked at both women as if to say, *You sure about this?*

Sophie nodded towards the lock and he turned.

"Let's get you something to drink," Sophie said nonchalantly as she pointed toward the couch. Vanessa sat.

"But what if I don't want anything to drink?"

Max leaned against the wall and watched the exchange.

"Believe me, you do need something to drink," Sophie shot back as she looked directly at Vanessa. She walked with a spiteful switch into the kitchen.

Vanessa slid her hand across her breasts as if to beckon Max. Max was cautious. He was waiting for Sophie to make the first move.

Sophie returned to the living room with two glasses of merlot. She handed one to Vanessa and sat down next to her.

"Nothing for me?" Max asked.

"If you want it, you're gonna have to come get it."

Sophie pointed her finger at Max and called him over slowly. She grabbed Vanessa's hair and cocked her head back.

"Look at that mouth. Ain't that a beautiful mouth?" Sophie kissed her.

Vanessa gyrated into the couch. Max kissed her neck and dragged his teeth along her jugular. He could feel her entire body pulsing against his lips. Sophie looked him in his eyes as she gently licked, then bit into Vanessa's lips.

Sophie unbuttoned her blouse as she kissed her.

Max was being extremely careful, at this moment he was just happy to be present. Sophie stood Vanessa up while taking off her own blouse. Vanessa smiled and looked away coyly. Max sat on the couch getting his voyeuristic fill. Sophie slipped out of her bra and brought Vanessa's mouth to her nipple. She looked at Max as Vanessa got a mouth-full of her breast. Vanessa moaned as she got excited.

Max took his shirt off and laid back in silence, his dick fully erect and shouting to the gods of all things primal. Sophie stepped out of her wide-legged cream pants, they fell to the floor like cherry blossoms. Vanessa slipped out of her sprawling African print skirt. The memories of her taste walked into Max's mouth. He stood and kissed her neck, then her shoulder, then slowly worked his way down her spine. He took his time to please every vertebra personally. Sophie reach down and gently passed her fingers through Vanessa vagina, and for a moment she paused. She had felt pussy before but this was something else.

Vanessa slowly pointed her toes towards each other and leaned into Sophie, they were breathing into each other's mouth while teasing with their tongues. Vanessa arched her back and elevated her ass so that Max could devour her. He bit into her ass cheek quietly then passed his nose up and down her thighs. He stopped about a hair's distance from the pleat of her vagina. She quivered.

Vanessa kissed Sophie as hard as she could, her juices squishing around inside of her. Sophie reached down and took Vanessa's leg into one arm, and as if they had planned it, Max slid his tongue into third base as he ducked beneath her raised leg and took her clit with all it's million nerve-endings into his mouth. Vanessa screamed as her juices gushed. Sophie felt her body trembling.

"Was that good?" Sophie whispered into her mouth.

"Oh, so good," Vanessa loved the way Sophie man-handled her.

It was as if Sophie was reading her mind and body. It was as if Sophie knew instinctively what she wanted.

"Are you a nasty little bitch?" Sophie said through her teeth.

Vanessa almost came again when Sophie said that.

"Yes, yes, I'm your nasty little bitch," her insides collapsed in on itself.

"No, no, you are not my nasty little bitch. Tonight you are Max's dirty little slut," Sophie said sternly as she pressed Vanessa's head into the couch, her ass hoisted in the air.

"Ooooooooohh, I am, I am." Vanessa mumbled into the cushion.

Sophie snapped her finger and Max was ready with condom slipped all the way down to the hilt of his dick.

"Max, I want you to fuck her like she has never been fucked before."

Sophie could feel a billion watts of sexual energy galloping through all her secret parts.

Vanessa writhed as she waited for Max to enter her. Max entered her as slowly as he could. He locked lips with Sophie as he went deeper and deeper.

Vanessa rotated her waist and pushed back as she moaned like wild woman. Max closed his eyes and said a prayer in every living language, to all the possible gods that have ever existed. He grasped Vanessa's waist as he stroked her.

Sophie slapped Vanessa's ass for effect.

"You love that dick?"

"Yes, yes, I love this dick?"

"Who are you?"

"Max's dirty little slut."

"And who am I?"

"I, I, I don't Know."

"I am your owner."

When those words hit Vanessa's ear she was a new woman. How did Sophie know exactly what she needed to hear? Her entire body was covered with goose pimples. She started shaking uncontrollably.

Max could feel his orgasm building. Sophie's control and power aroused him to the point where he felt his physical body hit an arousal wall.

Max was hitting all the right notes, all the right chords. Sophie was the maestro, the impresario. So everyone was shocked when in the throes of her oncoming orgasm, with her entire being rapt in passion, Vanessa screamed out, "Oh my god Maaaaaaaaax."

And just like that Sophie snapped, "What the fuck did you just say bitch?"

"Nothing, nothing, nothing."

The entire room stopped. Max felt it. Vanessa thought Sophie was still playing. Sophie realized that she felt jealousy. She had not felt jealous in such a long time, it was a new feeling. In the back of her head she tried to snap out of it. But it was lingering there.

Vanessa's face was pressed into the cushion. Max was behind her moving like he was about to enter another dimension.

Sophie grasped Vanessa's hair tighter, then whispered into her ear, "don't you ever fucking say his name again, you hear me bitch?"

And just like that, Vanessa exploded. Max exploded. And Sophie felt accomplished. Everything was wet, juices and sweat covered everything. Everything.

Chapter Twenty-Three

The following morning Max and Sophie were splayed in bed. The sun crept through the window and reminded them of their exploits the previous night. Sophie shook Max.

"Where's Vanessa? Did She leave?"

"I think she's on the couch."

Max did not know what to do.

In the bylaws of *The Threesome Handbook*, it is not the job of the home-owner to tell the third person in a threesome to leave. Good threesome etiquette prescribes that all third parties shall, without any prompting, exit the locale of said threesome immediately following *The Act*. Breakfast the following morning should never be assumed.

"What's that Max?" Sophie whispered.

"What's what?" Max cocked his head to listen for what Sophie was referencing.

"You smell that?" Sophie sat up in the bed.

"Is she cooking?" Max's mouth fell open.

There was an almost inaudible knock on their room door. They both froze. Before they could get themselves together, Vanessa pushed the room door open. She had made them breakfast. She was wearing an apron that said world's greatest chef. In the daylight she was threateningly beautiful. So beautiful it hurt a bit. She placed the try on the bed between Max and Sophie.

"I just wanted to say thank you," she shrugged and walked away like she owned the entire universe.

Something clicked inside of Max and Sophie at the same time.

"Hold on, come, come, come have some of this breakfast with us," Sophie said in a muted tone.

Vanessa paused in the doorway. She wanted to let them enjoy the rear-view for a few more seconds. Little did they know that the breakfast was a trap. She had gotten up and peeked into their room, saw them sleeping and decided she wanted another round. She was planning on having them for breakfast.

She turned and smiled with so much devil in her grin she could taste the fires of hell on her tongue; *and Bang*.

Chapter Twenty-Four

Amanda and Maurice were at war. They had been at war for over a year. That episode on the roof was seared into Maurice's psyche. Unlike most wars, this war was a silent war. They never spoke to each other unless they had to. When their daughter was around, you could not tell that they were at war. But kinds are much smarter than the people who make wars.

They were always smiles and sweet compliments which were a proxy for bitter and vengeful digs at each other. Maurice was constantly seething. Amanda was always playing defense. Every now and then he would drop an unsolicited remark.

"You fucking fucked Max!"

Then he would scoff and tramp off. Amanda would just pretend she did not hear his comment.

"Did you enjoy it?"

He would ambush her as often as he could.

Amanda did not really care what he felt or what he thought. He had made his bed.

They sat at the breakfast table having a nice American breakfast, with the sweet sounds of Saturday morning waltzing through the beautiful home they had built together.

Amanda paused for a moment as Miles Davis' Kind of Blue took over her being. Their beautiful daughter was busying herself with her plate of eggs and bacon, with not a single care in the world. Maurice's face seemed to be plotting his next verbal assault.

"I can't do this anymore Maurice," Amanda said the words as if she was speaking to herself. As if they had just happened upon her tongue. As if the words meant nothing.

"Wha, what?" Maurice was acting as if he did not know these words would eventually come.

Their beautiful daughter was frozen in place, mid chew, her mouth slammed open with surprise. The enormity of Amanda's statement sliced her in half. Amanda saw the look on her daughter's face and immediately the thought riffled through her mind, *Fuck I just turned my daughter into a stripper*.

Maurice quietly put his fork down and got up from the table. He had known the words were coming and he had prepared himself for the impact but he had no idea it would be this emotional. Even though he had been a shit husband and he knew he did not deserve Amanda's love, something inside of him was hurting.

He walked into the living room a sat on the couch and quietly wept. Amanda saw him sitting on the couch with his body filled with sadness and had a flash of the day Max had her arched, positioned, oiled up and bent over. Her insides quivered at the thought.

Chapter Twenty-Five

"Yeah, I go by Young Kevlar now."

"But why?"

"Because, I gotta switch the game up."

"Is that like the way Puff Daddy has a ton of names?"

"Kinda, but different."

"What's the difference?"

"Puff Daddy can't rap fo' shit."

"But he don't have to rap, he writes checks, ok."

"Shut up."

"But he does."

"He does but that is the corniest line EVER."

"Whatever, you just jealous you did not write it. So, what's up with this Marla chick, she still trying to fuck you?"

"Nah, I dead-ed that shit."

"Did you?"

"Yeah," KEV said quietly.

Marla can never be dead-ed.

"I don't believe that shit."

"You don't have to believe it, for it to be the truth."

"I don't trust you to tell the truth," Daren said in a very disgusted tone.

"I don't give a fuck if you trust me or not, but that's the truth."

KEV felt a kind of ease with Daren that he had never felt with another human being. Daren made him feel like himself. He did not have to pretend. He closed his eyes, placed his hands behind his head and sighed. Daren reached over and slid his hand gently across Young Kevlar's chest, as the morning sun greeted them in bed.

"So you leaving now, or what?"

"Damn, that's how you gon' treat me?"

"What you mean, you know you just a jump off right?"

Daren felt it to his core but he knew somewhere in there KEV was just playing. He shrugged it off.

"Whatever, you know you want me to stay."

"No, you have to leave. I'm serious bro," KEV was extremely blunt.

He needed Daren to leave because he wanted to be alone. He wanted to spend the rest of the day in this dope ass hotel suite that he booked for him and Daren. He wanted some selfcare.

"Listen man, I just wanna spend some time alone."

Daren kissed his teeth and rolled himself out of the bed and started the difficult task of squeezing into his skinny jeans.

"This will be the last time a lame like you get to... you know what, let me shut up."

"Do that ma dude."

KEV hated the fact that he had to live this double life. The truth is he wanted Daren gone because Daren was just a reminder of the one thing he could not be in this world. He kind of hated Daren for it. Hated him because Daren was able to be himself. He hated hip hop, he hated the hood, he hated the country. He was overwhelmed with anger. He felt something click inside his body. His face was wet. Why was he crying? Why was the world so cruel? He got rid of the tear before Daren could see it.

"I'm leaving," Daren was hoping he could find a way to stay.

He went an octave higher, "I'm leaving."

"Ok, I'll hit you up man," KEV said under his breath.

As soon as Daren exited KEV started shaking as he fell into a torrent of uncontrollable crying.

Chapter Twenty-Six

There are some relationships that will always exist. No matter how much chaos is thrown into the mix. Sometimes people are just attracted to each other and no rules, no laws or norms can prevent them from being together.

"So, you are telling me that you are no longer attracted to me sexually?"

"Well it's not that simple. I am attracted to you, it's just that I am not able to enjoy sex with you because I care about you, because I love you."

"That is the weirdest thing I have ever heard," Max was in a bowl of confusion.

His brain was having a hard time trying to understand what Sophie had just said.

"Ok, let me see if I can say it another way," Sophie looked up at the ceiling as she got her thoughts together.

"I am attracted to you, always have been, but what I have learned from my therapist is that I have to pretend to be someone else to really enjoy having sex with you. I have to pretend I am someone else to get past what my brain and body are telling me. My brain will not allow me to enjoy sex with you, as me, because I care about you."

Max was dumbfounded. His mouth was agape.

"So, all these years we were having sex you were pretending you were someone else?"

"No, Max," Sophie thought for a few seconds.

She took Max's hands, "I was not enjoying all those years of sex Max."

Her words hit him like a sword through his heart, "What? All those years?"

"Yes, all those years."

"So why didn't you say something?"

"I didn't even know I had an issue."

"Damn," Max was destroyed.

All those years and he thought he was doing something, he thought he was putting down that thang. He just knew he was a fantastic lover. Max felt as if he was watching himself getting his head chopped off.

"But, we are having the best sex now," Sophie assured him, "I just needed to tell you because I don't want us to hide anything from each other anymore."

"I hear you, I hear you." Max was still trying to make sense of everything Sophie had just dropped in his lap.

Sophie was looking at him like a new animal. She understood men and she knew this was going to affect him in a negative way for a bit but it was the best thing for their relationship.

Max stood up and walked towards the bathroom. He washed his face then looked at himself in the mirror. He was going over his entire sex life with Sophie. Then he thought about Amanda. Was it the same with her, was she not enjoying sex with him?

"So you're saying not even once?" He shouted from the bathroom.

Sophie walked towards the bathroom, by the time she hit her third stride she was a different person. She was no longer Sophie.

"I think I know what you want."

She looked over his shoulder into his eyes through the mirror, while sliding her hand across the front of his pants.

She kept whispering in his ears, "I want you to come all over my face."

Max was immediately aroused. She slid down onto her knees and took him into her mouth. And in that moment Max's brain was flooded with a dirty, dirty thought. He was getting sucked off by a stranger. *I should ask her to cry*, he thought to himself. And before he could stop himself. He grabbed her by the neck gently and looked her in her eyes, "Who are you?" he asked as if she was not Sophie.

"I'm your whore," she looked up at him with puppy dog eyes.

Strangely the vulnerability in her eyes aroused Max even more. He pulled his dick out of her mouth, "You want this dick?"

"Yes, please give me that big veiny cock," she was whimpering as she begged.

"I need you to beg for this dick to the point of tears, you hear me?"

"Please, oh, please give me that cock," she was begging like a crack fiend.

Her eyes filled with tears. Max felt a rush of devilry scream its way through his body like a beautiful nightmare. Every muscle in his body was taut as she took him into her mouth and worked his dick with a frenzied look in her eyes. And just when he was about to come, she stopped, looked up at him as if she was the most helpless creature on the planet, and said, "Come on my face;" *and Bang*.

Chapter Twenty-Seven

Ms. Clearmont loved new clients. They were like new projects. Her warm cozy office was an oasis locked away from the turmoil of New York City.

When Max entered the small office it immediately felt like home. It felt familiar. This was his first time going to see a therapist. He was desperately in search of answers. His heart was in his throat. Ms. Clearmont's smile eased a little bit of his tension but did not stop his mind from trembling. All he kept thinking was, what would his boys say if they found out he was at a therapist. Max was pretty progressive but going to a therapist was right at the line of not being in control of one's self, at least that's what he thought. It's right at the line of being insane. Max was willing to risk being found out to get to the bottom of what he was going through. He needed answers.

"So, tell me, have you been to therapy before?"

"No ma'am."

"You can call me Ms. Clearmont."

"Ok," he somehow lost his confidence.

This environment was relaxing but Max was nervous. He took a deep breath and tried to shake the feeling that was on him. He could hear the clock racing toward oblivion or wherever it is that clocks race to. He scanned the wall of books that were behind Ms. Clearmont.

"Tell me Max, what's your issue? What's bothering you? What's on your mind?"

He hesitated for a second. He should just tell her straight out, she was a professional. She would understand. His brain was whizzing in every direction.

"I have been having nightmares."

"Nightmares? What kind of nightmares?" Ms. Clearmont said warmly, her head tilted to the side.

"I keep having these nightmares about getting killed by one of my friends."

"By one of your friends?" She was curious.

Ms. Clearmont could tell this was not the reason why he was there but she would go along with him.

"Yes, an old friend from college."

"Why do you think you are having these nightmares about him?"

"I don't know."

Ms. Clearmont knew he was lying. His voice went up an octave, a clear sign that he was trying to hide something.

"But, he is your friend, right?"

"Yes, kinda, but we haven't been talking for a while and," Max paused for a moment.

His thoughts went back to room 809 at Aloft Brooklyn, Amanda weeping her eyes out.

"We kinda fell apart like a year ago because things got crazy, so maybe that's it."

"How did things get crazy?"

"You know thing just got crazy."

"Yes, I know how things can get crazy but what I want to know is how they got crazy."

A thousand episodes came crashing into Max's brain, and in every single episode he is fucking Amanda. He looked up at Ms. Clearmont.

"Yes, everything you say here is confidential," she said quietly.

And with that she sat back.

Chapter Twenty-Eight

It's difficult being straight in a straight world. So imagine the dilemma of Young Kevlar. He has only ever known two things for certain. One, that he wanted to be a rapper, and two that he was not like all the other boys. But in a world that says he couldn't exist as himself, he found ways to strive. He decided at a very young age to out-boy every boy he knew. To out-tough every male in his life.

He battled all the men his mother dated. He fought all his cousins. He got in more trouble than was necessary for a child. He was kicked out of every school in Brooklyn, then half of the school in Queens.

He loved the streets. He joined a gang when he turned thirteen. Before he knew it, he was one of the leaders. He hated his mother for having a different every year. He hated all the straight boys who got to be normal.

His mother kicked him out the house his senior year of high school. She said it was because he was in a gang, but he knew better. He knew it was because she did not want him having boys at the house, influencing his younger brother. She was having none of it, especially since that one episode that almost tore their family apart during the summer before his senior year.

His mother was old school. She was from the south and something about god and whatever else. She couldn't love her son, her flesh and blood because he was different. He was not the way the lord intended.

Chapter Twenty-Nine

Maurice walked the few short blocks from The Emerson to The Five Spot. It was barely eight in the evening. It was still bright out and the summer was fragrant around him. He was scheming on ways he could get back at Max. He could hear the blood cooking in his veins.

He walked into The Five Spot knowing he was going to see Maybeline. They had been hooking up on and off for the past year. He had not seen her in about a month, he was fiending for her. So when he got the text to stop by, he knew it was on. Yeah, she was not his type, but she fucked lightyears better than his type. That one gold front vanished when he entered her, or when she placed both palms on his chest and rode him like an old mule.

Maurice walked into the airconditioned lounge and left the weight of the summer outside. He slid up to the bar and ordered his regular, a vodka cranberry. Maybeline served him and acted as if she did not know him.

"I get off in thirty minutes," she was always very direct.

He had been her own little plumber, her own little handy man for the past year and she had no qualms about asking for what she wanted, when she wanted it. It was one of those mutually beneficial situations. They did not ask each other many questions. They met, they fucked, and then they would go their way until the next time.

"You want me to meet you there?"

"Yeah, that works."

Maurice had about four drinks. He gave Maybeline a huge tip.

"That's way too much money for a tip," she slid forty dollars back to him.

He wanted her to have the entire hundred, but she was having none of it.

She wiped down the bar as the sun fell from the sky. Her replacement walked in just as she finished.

"Meet me in like fifteen minutes, I have to tidy up a bit," Maybeline said with a wink and a smile.

Maurice hung back for a bit and had another drink, then walked over. He entered the aromatics of her small apartment and knew Maybeline had planned something special for him. There were candles everywhere. If he did not know better, he might think she was trying to set the apt on fire. When he saw the tiny cake on her dining table it occurred to him that it was her birthday.

Maybeline had drawn a bath and wanted Maurice to get in the tub with her. The tub was an atrocity, but it was her birthday so he obliged.

They sat in the dingy tub facing each other. She reached for his dick and felt it swelling in her palm.

"Let's go to the bedroom."

He followed her, his body dripping with water.

"Lay on your stomach."

He laid on his stomach.

"Give me on second, I have to go get something."

Maurice did not know what she had planned but he decided to play along. He heard the microwave go ping in the kitchen.

She straddled his back as if she was going to give him a massage.

"This is gonna be a little cold."

"Cold?"

Maurice though she was getting warm wax or something like that.

"It's just ice-cream."

"Ice-cream? What are you doing with Ice-cream?

"Shhhhh," she wanted him to relax.

She gently poured it between his shoulder blades and down his entire back then between his ass cheeks. Then she licked it all up. By the time she got to the small of his back his ass was in the air waiting. In his mind he knew he was violating every rule of being a man but he could not control himself. The molten ice-cream slid across his taint and around his balls. She slid her tongue through his ass and took his spirit out of his body. She paused, caught her breath, then went back for a mouth full of balls. Maurice quivered on the bed.

"You ok baby?" She mumbled licking the ice-cream from her lips.

"Hm mm," his eyes were filled with tears.

She poured more of the ice-cream into his ass and went back for seconds. He was face down, ass up in the bed, looking like a baby elephant kneeling. She rolled him over and took the entirety of his dick into her mouth. She licked every drop of ice-cream from every inch then spat it back onto his dick then slurped it back into her mouth. Maurice did not want to admit it but he knew inside that this old woman had just turned him out.

Chapter Thirty

Emily was worried, she had been texting Brenton all evening and he had not replied. Brenton stood outside of Emily's door trying to think of an excuse. Why was he late? He lived only a few blocks away. He pressed the bell. Emily was livid.

She did not say anything at first. The dinner she had prepared was cold. There was nothing that he could say that could fix this. She hated nothing more than a person who was late. The only thing she hated more was a person who lied about being late.

"What happened?" She said in a testy voice.

"You want the truth?" He said widening his eyes.

"That would be a good start," she was annoyed.

"I fell asleep at this girl's house."

"At a girl's house? Really? You expect me to believe that?" She just knew he was lying.

"Ok, ok, you caught me, I was out with KEV at Bed Vyne drinking," he dropped his head.

"I fucking knew it, you could have fucking called me." She chucked him by the shoulder.

"I know, I know, it's just that sometimes when you're out it's hard to stop drinking."

She looked at him with questioning eyes. They hug.

"So, guess what I made?"

"I don't know, what?"

"Your favorite."

Brenton cringed. Since he had been dating her he had lost quite a few pounds, mainly because she did not know how to cook.

"Yum."

She smiled, she loved cooking for Brenton. They sat on the floor of her living room and had a picnic. They ate and spoke quietly.

"Babe, do you like my cooking," she said with deep reservation.

"I," he paused.

He wanted to be truthful but he knew it would destroy her.

"I do, but not as much as I love you," he kissed her on the lips.

"I feel like you don't like my cooking," she said introspectively, "you never rave about it."

"True, but your food it mostly for nutrition, not particularly for raving."

"So what would make you rave about it?"

"What would make me rave about it? What would make me rave about it?" Brenton was searching.

"It's pretty hard to make asparagus and salmon with corn on the side worthy of raving, huh?" She had trapped him.

"Well yes and no, I think if you used a little bit more seasoning it would be amazing."

"Jonathan loved my cooking," she accidentally blurted out.

Brenton smiled, "but we are different people."

"I'm sorry babe, I shouldn't have said that."

"No, it's fine. Y'all were together for a long time so I see how..."

"No, no there's no reason I should be judging what you like by what someone else liked."

"See, that's why I love you."

They kissed and their picnic slowly turned into moans.

Chapter Thirty-One

Marla and KEV were a strange pair. She was a fan first, but in the last six months or so she had parlayed their friendship into a personal assistant career. She was his gatekeeper. She decided the who, the when, and the where.

KEV was a mob boss and she was his consiglieri. Every now and then she would get jealous about the life he was living. There were women everywhere and at every turn she had to check them. She had grown accustomed to hearing KEV having sex with this one or that one but she kept her feelings where they needed to be as one who understood her position of power and privilege.

"So can I come over this evening?"

"I don't know. What's poppin?" KEV was barely interested.

"I just wanna hang, plus I have a gift and a friend I want to introduce to you," she dragged out the ending of the word hang.

That was their code, which meant she wanted to smoke. A gift meant she had a new strain of weed she wanted him to try out, and a friend to meet meant she had a friend she wanted him to meet.

KEV leaned back into his couch and looked at his blunt, he smiled. There was more weed coming.

"Yeah, come through."

Marla was excited. Her friend Maria did not believe that she knew KEV let alone worked for him.

"What kinda gift you got though?"

"Oh, you are gonna love this, Alien Kush, it's a hybrid indica mix."

KEV loved the fact that Marla knew all this detailed information about weed. She was trying to educate him on all the different strains and what they were good for, even though he just wanted to get high.

"How about your friend, she cute?"

Marla looked Maria up and down.

"She is sexy, tanned, dark hair..."

"Say less, ma dude."

Marla hated when KEV called her *ma dude*. KEV called all women in his circle, *ma dude*; *and Bang*.

KEV has an eternity of smoke bellowing out of his face. He could feel the potency moving through his body. He was relaxed. He licked, then sucked on the blunt one more time then exhaled. The smoke hugged the walls.

Maria had a million questions. KEV was not willing to answer a single one. He just wanted to enjoy his high.

"I thought you said he was fun," Maria was a little upset.

"He is, he's just busy right now," Marla whispered.

KEV's phone rang. It was Daren. He looked at his phone while Maria sat on the floor next to him. He passed her the blunt.

"Why, are you answering your phone? That's disrespectful," Maria was offended.

"Disrespectful?" He looked at her like she had ten heads.

She smacked the phone out of his hand. KEV looked at Marla like she had brought the devil into his apartment.

"Marla, get ya girl."

Marla gave Maria a stern look. Maria returned the look.

"What? You wanna see these," Maria waved her chest at KEV, trying to get his attention.

KEV got up from the couch and continued speaking into the phone.

Marla slapped Maria on her breast, "Put those away."

She slowly tucked them back where she had gotten them.

Chapter Thirty-Two

Marla and Maria are sitting sluggishly in KEV's living room casually watching TV under a blanket. KEV is standing by the window watching a young couple arguing across the street from his apartment building, he is quietly laughing and talking into his phone.

Brenton and Emily are sitting in the middle of the meadow in Prospect Park. Brenton is not a big fan parks but Emily was persistent. He is slowly finding out that the outdoors can be amazing.

Sophie and Meghan are sitting across from each other at Saraghina. Saraghina sits on the corner of Lewis and Halsey. It looks like an old garage converted into a pizza restaurant. It is as rustic as you can get without being condemned by the city of New York. It has a kind of charm that theoretically should be a turn off but it works in that particular space. The tables and chairs are all miss-matched. The floor is made out of pieces of the middle ages. The staff are friendly and the food is good, so it's always packed.

Daren's phone pinged to life. His screen lit up. It was a message from Sheila. It simply said, *WE NEED TO TALK*.

Daren studied the message. He scrolled through their interaction a few nights back to see what the issue could be. He kept coming up with Nothing. Maybe it was the kiss? Maybe she wanted to see if they could work something out?

Maurice had both hands clamped onto Maybeline's hips as he pumped his way to yet another dishonorable orgasm. He wiped the sweat from his brow as he grunted in slow motion.

"Give me that nasty dick you dirty motherfucka," Maybeline was an exceptional coach. She brought things out of Maurice he did not know he had. Her dirty talk kept him hard even after he came.

Max was in his apartment thumbing through his Instagram page when his door bell rang. He had no idea who it could be. He looked through the peep hole and was shocked to see Vanessa there. His mouth fell open. *What is she doing here?* He thought. He immediately went to the mayhem of their last encounter. He opened the door and just as he did a message came onto the screen of his phone. It was from Amanda.

Trace and Victoria were on some random sidewalk arguing about whether or not Trace loved her, whether or not they should take their relationship to the next level. Trace was frustrated. He was new to the city and he did not want a commitment just yet. Victoria was thirty-four years old so she did not have the time for games anymore. For her it was really simple.

"Why are you making things so complicated? It's either, I'm the one or I'm not."

"It not that simple Victoria. I really, really like you, yeah. But I think we are rushing things."

Victoria could hear her life ticking away. She was not going to spend another year or two hoping Trace came around.

Chapter Thirty-Three

Marla slides her feet under the covers towards Maria warm crotch. She was still all squishy on the insides. Marla gently pressed her toes into Maria's thigh. Maria looked at Marla and smiled mischievously at her. She slid her hand beneath the covers and took Marla's feet and pressed it gently into the mouth of her vagina and humped her toes slowly.

KEV was texting back and forth with Daren. He had two naked women on his couch but all he could think about was Daren. Daren was his peace.

He had no desire to be laid up with Marla and Maria, sharing stories about his dreams and his aspirations. Like most things in his life, women were a facade. He did what he had to do to keep who he was from leaking out.

"So, can I come by?" Daren wanted to know.

"Nah, not right now, I have a meeting with my assistant and some people who are trying to bring me down to Miami."

"When then, how about later?"

"Later sounds good, I'll text you."

"Ok cool."

He turned around to find Marla and Maria with their eyes closed. Marla's mouth half agape with her lips trembling while Maria was in a full eye-roll and a micro shriek.

"What the fuck y'all doing?"

They were both startled.

Marla called KEV over.

KEV smiled and shook his head.

"Nah, I'm good. I'll watch tho."

He re-lit his blunt and thought about Daren.

Maria raised one eyebrow at Marla; *and Bang*.

Chapter Thirty-Four

The machine that is Saraghina was buzzing all around Sophie and Meghan, but their focus was so intense you would not have known all this chaos was right at their fingertips.

"I tried everything Sophie, but it seems like everything I do is not enough."

"But what is his hang up?"

"He thinks that I don't dress like a woman of the cloth."

"A woman of the cloth? What is that supposed to mean?"

"I don't know, he thinks that the people in the church are talking behind his back about the way I dress."

"What kind of a church is that, where people talk behind your back about the way you dress?"

"Well, seems like all of them?"

"Aren't they supposed to be the good people, who take you as you are?"

"Yeah, they all say that."

Then they both say in unison, "But they don't live it."

They laughed for a few moments.

Meghan hesitated for a second. She mulled over what she was about to say to Sophie. She closed her eyes, took a deep breath and then sighed.

"You wanna know the worst thing about him trying to live up to these peoples' standards."

Sophie sensed a bowl of secrets coming, "What?" She leaned in.

"They're all hypocrites, and I have the receipts."

"You do? How?" Her eyes widened.

"Girl listen," Meghan was old school Meghan from a year ago, Meghan before she found Jesus Meghan. Her tone alone told Sophie that she was back. Meghan hesitated again.

"I'm listening," Sophie made the sign for sipping tea and smiled as she did so.

"They are so hypocritical and I'm going to expose them all."

"Girl, stop fucking beating around the bush and tell me," Sophie wanted all the Juicy details.

Meghan was about to open up a door into what had been going on with her and members of the church. Sophie's eyes were saying, *give it to me*, but she was not ready for what was coming.

Chapter Thirty-Five

Daren whispered cautiously into his phone. He was standing in the foyer at the exact spot where he had last had sex with Sheila, if he could call it sex. The way he remembered it, everything was a blur.

"What is this about?

"We just really need to talk."

"But I don't know what we would be talking about."

"I don't want to talk about it on the phone Daren."

"What could be so pressing that you can't say it on the phone?

"Where are you Daren?"

"I'm at my cousin Amanda's," Daren moved outside as he spoke.

He did not want Amanda or Maurice in his business. He was getting angry about Sheila's secrecy.

"I'm coming by."

"What?" Daren was peeved.

How dare she just decide to show up without his consent?

An Uber pulled up outside Maurice and Amanda's home. The heat was in a fuss. The humidity was in a rancorous mood. The wind sat about just breathing heavy on everything.

Daren opened the door slightly and spoke through the crack.

"What's up?" He looked Sheila up and down.

Sheila reached into her purse and handed him a pregnancy test. Daren took it from her as if it was an alien object from another universe.

"It says pregnant," he looked at her with his brow knitted.

Sheila was shaking her head, she had a look of sad excitement on her face. She was waiting for a cue from Daren. She gestured with both hands.

"But, how?"

"What do you mean? Three weeks ago we ..." Sheila had a dumbfounded look on her face.

Daren played the tape through his head of the last time they hooked up; *and Bang*.

He slapped his hand over his mouth, his eyes almost popped out of his head. They had had unprotected sex. The entire universe came crashing into Daren's body.

"Oh Fuck."

Chapter Thirty-Six

Meghan looked around the restaurant, as if she was about to tell Sophie the location of the Holy Grail. Sophie could barely contain herself.

"So, when I first went to the church, I was still dressing how I used to dress. I would always get these looks from the people in the church, especially the church board. I knew they were talking about me, but really I didn't give a fuck, excuse my French," Meghan was in between worlds.

Sophie saw the disdain in her eyes.

"Emmanuel didn't care either way but the church board kept telling him that since he was the junior pastor, *HE* needed to make sure his woman was more respectable," Meghan rolled her eyes.

"Wow, they went straight for the jugular," Sophie understood the ways of the black church very well.

"Yeah, they did, it almost broke us up. To be honest, I kinda knew at that point Emanuel and I wouldn't last."

"It did? What? How did you come to that conclusion?"

"Yeah, he's so into all that church stuff, but he's also so good in bed," Meghan paused.

"I hear that," Sophie smiled.

"Anyway, I decided to play their little game. I changed my wardrobe completely. But I had a plan. I knew they were not as righteous as they said they were," Meghan had a soft vengeance in her voice.

"So, what did you do?"

"I started this project of testing the members of the board."

"How did you test them?" Sophie leaned in as she whispered.

Meghan scanned the room again, "I fucked them all."

"You what?" Sophie almost lost her mind.

"Yes, I fucked every last one of them."

Sophie stood up and walked away from the table for a second. She did not know what to do with what she just heard. It was insane, it was unthinkable, but it was so, so, so scandalous.

Sophie came and sat back down, "You what?"

Meghan closed her eyes and gently said, "Fucked. Them. All. Girl."

Chapter Thirty-Seven

Meghan's first target was Deacon Matthews. He was in his early forties, ambitious, well dressed and utterly unfulfilled. You could see it in his walk. He was just waiting for someone to die so he could move up in the church ranks.

Deacon Matthews was married. His wife was perfect. His children were perfect. They were the envy of the entire congregation. At second glance though you could see the threads pulling apart, you could see the mayhem screaming to be released.

So, as if Meghan had planned it, Deacon Matthews asked her if she was going to come to bible study the following Wednesday. As soon as the words came out his mouth, Meghan knew it. *Oh, mister holy man,* she thought, *I think I got you where I want you.* Meghan paused, smiled and took his prayer meeting pamphlet; *and Bang*.

She is hanging upside down in a hotel room, her hair sweeping the floor, her mouth filled to the brim with the forbidden heft of Deacon Mattews' Dick. His biceps are wrapped around her thighs, holding her in place as he eats his way to the juicy center of her holy book. He was like a wild man eating for the first time in years. Meghan had had her pussy eaten many different ways before, but his intensity and veracity were scary.

He stuck his nose in it. He spat in her ass, slurped the spit out, then spat it back. The splatting sound was like a shot of adrenaline that ran up her spine. The chemicals in her body raged and screamed and called out to god and begged for his forgiveness.

Deacon Mattews fucked her like a convict, like a man sentenced for eating another human being, like a gorgon who had just come up out of the sea to devour an entire village of screaming women.

She had to calm him down a few times.

"Relax babe, I'm gonna be here. I am not going anywhere."

"Oh, sorry, sorry it's just that I have not had sex-sex in like 6 years," he was earnest and formal about his desires.

The air conditioner in the newly fashioned hotel on Atlantic Avenue kept a steady flow of cool air circulating. Meghan drained every drop of fluid from his body and left him in the hotel room to figure out his esteemed morals.

Chapter Thirty-Eight

Sophie's eyes were ready to roll out of their sockets. Her mouth wide open.

"So, hold up," she couldn't even put two thoughts together.

Her brain was like the Indy 500 except the cars were going in both directions.

"You fucked the deacon? Isn't he like close friends with Emmanuel?"

"He's one of Emmanuel's closest friends, but I wanted to prove a point. "

"And what point is that?"

"I needed to prove to Emmanuel that his church people are not as holy as he thinks they are."

"Well damn girl, there must have been another way to prove your point," Sophie was shocked but the details were too juicy to get into morals.

Chapter Thirty-Nine

Fabiola Ransom is beautiful. She was punishingly beautiful. Fabiola Ransom was overbearingly sexy. She has always been sexy. She never got married because Jesus was the only man she needed. She poured her entire life into the church. Her mind, body and spirit belong to the lord.

The first time Fabiola Ransom saw Meghan she hated every bone in her body. Meghan exuded all the things that Fabiola had been keeping tucked away from the public. How could this young girl, child really, walk into her church like she was a sex goddess. Something burned inside of her because Meghan was like a mirror. All the sexy things that Fabiola had been hiding started showing up in her emotions, and that was not good.

So, it was not by accident that one evening Fabiola invited Meghan over to her one bedroom apt to talk about Meghan getting more involved in the inner workings of the church.

Meghan had played all her cards perfectly. She had dropped the idea in Emmanuel's head knowing it would end up with her fingering Fabiola on her exquisitely Christian couch.

The moment Meghan walked through the door she could feel the swelling feeling of Fabiola's cravings. She could feel the sexual energy climbing the walls and humping the pillows on her love seat. Fabiola was dressed like she was prepared for church, pencil skirt, floral blouse and kitten heels. Meghan was casual, jeans and a slinky top. She wore no underwear, for a very specific reason. Fabiola fought with all her might. She offered tea. She offered water. She offered a snack.

"I would love a snack," Meghan replied to her offer.

Fabiola knew the ways of the devil. If she was not a woman of god who did not like casting judgements, she would think Meghan was inferring that she, Fabiola Ransom, should be the snack, which was thoroughly inappropriate. She brushed off the thought.

Fabiola went to the kitchen and came back with two plates with cookies. She placed them nimbly in front of Meghan. Meghan smiled on the inside, here she was in the home of her target and what did her target bring her, cookies.

Next, Fabiola placed two short glasses of orange pineapple juice in front of Meghan.

"You know what they say about pineapple juice right?"

"Girl, you know I don't know nothing bout no pineapples," Fabiola tried to laugh off the discomfort.

"They say it makes your coochie taste great," Meghan said in a slick tone.

"Well, I would not know anything about that, it's just me and ma Jesus, so...," she looked off to the right.

Fabiola could feel the tiny rumblings in her vagina.

"Jesus? Jesus takes care of the spirit. Who takes care of the body Fabiola?" Meghan said in her best church voice.

And maybe it's because she had been celibate for so long, or maybe it was the heat pushing it's nipples up against the window, or maybe something in Meghan's being had just triggered a deep, deep loneliness inside of her, but Fabiola's eyes welled up with tears.

"What's wrong?" Meghan inquired.

"I don't know," Fabiola was trying to laugh off the tears.

Meghan placed her palm on Fabiola's thigh to comfort her. And in that moment Fabiola paused and was quiet for a few seconds. She did not know what to do with the sexual rage she was feeling. She got up abruptly and went to the bathroom.

Meghan watched her ass as she carefully carried herself. She was in the bathroom a few minutes. When she came back to the couch, Meghan asked her to stand. She stood up and Meghan hugged her as tightly as she could.

For the first time in years Fabiloa had an intimate moment with another human being. They stood there hugged up in her living room for what seemed like an eternity.

As they were about to release each other, Meghan took a nostril full of Fabiola's fragrance. Her nose gently brushed Fabiola's neck; *and Bang*.

Fabiloa is huffing and panting and writhing and calling out the lord's name in vain, as Meghan's middle fingers are calling entire sections of heaven from her g-spot. Fabiola could feel the universe collapsing in on her. That's when Meghan took one final mouth full of her sumptuous breasts and slid down to her clit. Meghan licked her so gently that she lost her vision for a few moments. Her back arched upward toward the ceiling and she roared like a lion as she came. Meghan continued and Fabiola came again. Meghan kept at it and she came again.

Fabiola was trembling. She felt guilty. What had she done?

Meghan looked up at her all fragile and vulnerable and said, "Pineapples."

Chapter Forty

Meghan walked out into the summer humidity with her head held high. The heat greeted her like an old friend. They held hands as she waited for her Uber. She slid into the back seat and reflected on what had just happened. In the back of her mind she said, *two down, two to go*.

The Uber driver took her straight to the church. She had a meeting scheduled with the Youth Fellowship Director, Jeffery Patterson.

The Uber pulled up in front of the church, she could still taste Fabiola on her lips. Jeffery was in the basement, in his little youth office planning away.

It literally takes nothing for a young man barely out of college to lose faith in everything he believes in. His office was a jumbled and tight space, it was part office, part church pantry.

When Meghan walked in with sex oozing out of her pores like a mountain stream, Jeffery immediately got an erection.

"So, what do you need help with?" Meghan closed the door behind her.

He got up to shake her hand. Meghan saw his awkward erection. She saw his juvenile shame. He felt exposed. She smiled and took his hand. She looked him up and down. She could see that he did not have much living experience. She chuckled inside at his attempt at being confident.

"How old are you?"

"Ah, ah, twenty-three ma'am," his voice was shaking.

She pulled him closer and whispered into his ear, "Is anybody here besides you?"

He was confused, "Well, no... just... ah...today is Tuesday... I am just keeping office hours."

He was the hardest he had ever been in his life. At this moment she could have offered him a ticket straight to hell and he would have taken it.

She slowly unbuttoned her jeans, her eyes on him the whole time. He passed out in his spirit. And in his mind there was a time jump; *and Bang*.

Her breasts are pressed against the door of his tiny office and he is on his knees behind her, having the time of his life. He was licking and sucking and slurping like his life depended on it.

She slipped a condom on his over-eager dick and sat him down on a chair and went to work. She rode him like a young stallion who needed breaking. He came about a thousand times without losing his erection. She left all kinds of hickies and scratch marks all over his body to make a point.

"I think we should definitely do this again next Tuesday," she said as she fixed herself and walked out of his office.

He was still seated with his pants around his ankles.

He nodded, "We should, we should."

Chapter Forty-One

After preaching in the streets Emmanuel Cox was a mountain, he was a panther, he was the fifth dimension, he was an old phonograph playing backwards and forwards at the same time.

Preaching and handing out pamphlets after work brings him to life. He didn't know exactly why, but it did. Maybe it was all the rejection. Maybe it was all raucous energy around him or the nasty looks he got from non-believers. He did not care. All he knew was that after an evening of preaching on the subway or at Broadway Junction, he was his greatest self. He was fully realized. He was fulfilled. He could fuck like a god.

On those nights Meghan gave thanks for the level of attention he gave to her. She was a religious shrine and he had made his pilgrimage to pray at her alter. And pray he did.

He would start off with her toes and he would work his way up her entire body as slowly and as meticulously as he could. She would catch the holy ghost before he entered her, and when he entered her it was with all the things he was made of. When he was in her, he wasn't just inside of her with his dick, he was inside of her like a spiritual occupation. He was looking out through her eyes. His intensity in the bed matched his intensity on the trains when he was preaching. Amen.

Chapter Forty-Two

Daren and Sheila are sitting in the living room like two gravestones. Sheila is glaring at him questioningly. Daren did not know what to say. He never imagined he would be in this position. Here he is a gay man, caught up in a straight man's hell. Baby mamma drama? What the hell was happening to him? His world was upside down and sideways.

"Are you gonna keep it?" He asked inaudibly.

"What? What kind of question is that?"

"I honestly don't know what to say, I've never been in this situation before."

"Well, I have, and I don't think I want to go down that road again."

"So, does that mean you're gonna keep it?"

"I don't know Daren," Sheila was irritated.

They were quiet for a few second.

"It's still early, though," she said as if to herself.

Daren sensed an opening, "What do you mean it's still early?"

"If we decided to have an," she paused, "abortion. It's still early enough."

Daren felt hopeful.

"But I have been down that road and I'm getting up there in age and this might be my last chance."

"No it's not. I think you'll be fine. People are having babies later and later in life."

"But, so if I have it, would you be my support?"

"Have it like, if you keep it would I be your support?"

"Yes, my support."

Daren's face fell. He could barely take care of himself, how was he going to take care of her and a child? To make matters worse, Sheila did not even know that he was gay. What would she think if he told her now?

"I guess. I don't have a choice then, right?"

"Yes, you do, you just have to tell me what you want to do." Sheila sounded earnest.

"If I'm a hundred percent honest," he tried to catch her eye, "I would say let's not have it."

Sheila was heartbroken. She was hoping for a different answer.

"Wow," was all she could muster.

"I didn't mean it like that," he tried to caution her.

"How did you mean it."

Daren did not know what to say. He sat across from Sheila trying to disappear into the couch.

Chapter Forty-Three

Trace was in no place emotionally to have a conversation, but Victoria needed an answer.

"It's not gonna work," he said drily as he shrugged.

Victoria was happy he finally told her.

"Thank you, was that so hard? Huh? Was it?"

She was going to milk the situation for as long as she could. She knew he felt bad so she was going make sure his guilt ate him alive.

The evening was closing in on them. Trace saw a strange figure in an apartment across the street watching their argument.

"I guess you're gonna come get your stuff today," Victoria said matter-of-factly.

"No, I can't do today," Trace batted down the idea.

"What you got do?" She tried to get under his skin.

"I have some things to do."

"Well, if you don't come get your stuff today, I am putting them in the garbage," Victoria said distracted by her purse.

She took out her phone and started searching through numbers.

"Time to make new friends."

Trace felt the dagger push into his body.

"Damn, it's that real?" He was aghast.

"Yes, it is, you don't seem to understand that all of this is in high demand?" She gestured to her body.

"I never said I didn't want all of that. All I said was I'm not ready for a relationship right now," he pressed his finger into her side.

Victoria looked up at Trace longingly then quietly said, "Whatever;" *and Bang*.

Victoria is on top of Trace riding him like she was trying to break his dick off.

"You know you want this pussy. You know you love this fucking pussy. You ain't never going no fucking where," she accented the end of each sentence with a little something extra.

"Oh my god I fucking love this pussy. It's so juicy and tight and oh god."

Trace came.

Victoria was not going to let him off that easy. She took him in her mouth and worked on his dick until it was hard and glistening.

"There we go," she said as soon as her mouth was unoccupied.

This time she mounted him in reverse cowgirl and rode the life out of him. They woke up at midnight not knowing how they ended up in her bed.

Chapter Forty-Four

Daren was depressed. He went for a walk on Myrtle avenue. He was hoping he would get some great epiphany but it never came. For the first time in his life he needed to be responsible, but he just did not know how.

He called KEV.

"Sup?" KEV was in a cloud of smoke.

Maria and Marla had left. He was alone.

"I just need someone to talk to."

"To talk to?"

"Yeah," Daren sounded sincere.

KEV was not falling for that bullshit, "Nigga if you trying to fuck you don't have to do all that fancy shit with me."

Daren really wanted to talk but at the moment he would take whatever he could get; *and Bang*.

Daren is getting his lungs torn out by KEV. KEV was at his sexual pinnacle when he was with Daren. He was totally focused on the task at hand. He was so high and his head was filled with so much chaos that he felt like he had to break something. And Break he did.

When they finished, Daren was a new man. He had never been rage-fucked before. This was new. And he loved it.

KEV wanted him gone as soon as they were done.

"I guess I'll have to find someone else to talk to about my issues."

KEV knew he was being selfish. He did not want to be like that but he had to, he was beginning to care too much about Daren.

Chapter Forty-Five

It's early evening. There is a gentle breeze. Brooklyn is rarely cool in the summer. Days like this are the best.

Trace and Brenton are sitting at a table in Habana Outpost. They did not have anything to do but shoot the shit.

Brenton had a meeting with a new client at 8pm at The Brooklyn Moon so he had a ton of time to kill.

"What's that like bruv?" Trace wanted to know what if felt like to have an artist who was becoming one of the hottest things in music.

"It's cool, but it ain't my thing really," Brenton said in few syllables.

"What? You're kidding right?"

"No, not really man. When I started working with KEV he was underground. I felt like I was shaking things up. His talent was raw, it was pure. But now I feel like it's just a minstrel show."

"What, minstrel show? When that shit comes on in the club yeah? Everybody loses their shit, yeah? What are you talking about?"

"I don't know man, I'm just a little suspect about the direction his music is going."

"I hear you bruv but that money is proper, yeah?"

"Ahhhh, it's alright," Brenton hated talking about money with friends and family.

Brenton spotted Marla and her friend Maria walk in. He decided to play it cool. Let her come to him. He had a quick thought about the first time he met her. He smiled to himself.

"What's, what's going on," Trace saw the change in his face.

Trace looked around and spotted the two young women.

"Bruv...," Trace gave him the Black James Bond look.

Brenton did not want to be bothered.

"How's Victoria?"

"Victoria's good, we fight almost every day bruv."

"Damn. Everyday?"

"No, no, no, no it's a good thing."

"It is?"

"Yes, it is," Trace said with deep earnest.

"How?" Brenton needed to know.

"How do I explain this," Trace tried to be nuanced about his explanation. "Fuck it, I'll just be honest. I think we fight because it makes the sex better."

"What? Hold up, hold up. Are these real fights?"

"Yes."

"You have real fights so that your sex life can be better?"

Trace was quiet for a few seconds before he grimacingly admitted, "Yes, we kinda do mate."

"That's fucking insane."

"It is innit?"

"What do you fight about?" In Brenton's mind is there would not be enough things to fight about.

"We fight about everything mate."

"Everything?"

"Everything."

"Is it worth it?"

"You have no fucking idea. The sex is so primal and nasty afterwards, it's totally worth it."

"What's worth it?" Marla slide up next to Brenton.

Her friend stood next to her.

"Hey, Marla right? Just kidding. How are you?"

Marla immediately knew what the tone of his voice meant.

"Who is this?" Trace asked.

"This is my friend Marla and her friend Maria from Miami, this is my cousin Trace."

"Hey Trace nice to meet you," Marla slid her hand into his, and just like that, the entire world froze; *and Bang*.

Brenton, Trace, Marla and Maria are transported into Marla's apartment. There are clothes everywhere; on the floor, over the lamp in the corner, on her little Ikea chair, even atop her air-conditioning unit. Brenton is arched up behind Marla. She is on her knees. She is attempting to suck a historical document out of Trace's dick.

Maria is beneath Marla with Brenton's balls in her mouth while Trace waits to put down the magna carta. Marla slides a condom unto his dick with her mouth then guides the entire thing into Maria. The temperature of the room changed.

There is much moaning and screaming and panting and juices and scratches and slurping and pounding and ass slapping and dick wrangling. And for a second Brenton and Trace looked at each other and smiled. In their minds they high-fived each other.

"We're doing a Tower Bridge mate."

Marla looked up from her licking. She pushed Trace onto his back and jumped onto his Maria-creamed dick. And in that same moment as if they were synchronized, Maria pushed Brenton onto his back and climbed on board. Both women looked at each other and smiled.

"Race you to the finish line," Maria whispered across to Marla.

They both started riding as fast as they could. The music of their vaginas was like two snakes wrestling in a tub of oil. Brenton and Trace were trying their best not to come. This was a batte of wills. The sexual energy in the room was palpable, was electric.

Just when they were about to come Maria said, "switch;" *and Bang*.

Chapter Forty-Six

"We never speak of this again."

"My lips are sealed," Marla replied.

"I don't live here," Maria made a face as she spoke.

Brenton and Trace were almost dressed. Trace wanted to stay. Brenton was in a hurry to leave. He could see Trace dragging his feet.

"What if I just catch up with you later, after your meeting," Trace said, acting against code.

"It's up to you man, I got this meeting I have to get to."

"Ok cool, I'll catch you later."

"I thought you had a meeting about the account with Victoria Secrets."

Trace knew that Brenton was talking about Victoria. He was being stubborn. Marla and Maria pulled the sheets over their heads and pretended to moan.

"I cancelled that meeting mate."

Brenton narrowed his eyes, and mouthed the words, "Let's go."

"No, I'll stay."

"Ok cool, whatever *bruv*" Brenton could not understand what was going on with Trace.

Brenton walked out the door fuming.

Trace started undressing. Maria and Marla flung the sheet open. Trace was back in the bed in a second, fuck taking his clothes off. He just wanted to be up inside Marla and Maria and taking his clothes off was not required.

Chapter Forty-Seven

"**W**hat happened?" Max was dying to hear.

"Bro, it was crazy man. Me and Trace are sitting at Habana Outpost, and guess who walks in?

"Who?"

"Marla."

"Who's Marla again?"

Remember that white girl who used to work for Fader magazine, she was around all of last summer and no one could remember her name? The one I had that threesome with."

"Yeah, isn't she working with KEV now."

"Yeah, she's his personal assistant."

"Damn, mofuckas have PAs now."

"So it's her and her friend Maria from last year, so I'm like bet."

"Yeah, yeah now I remember, you left with them from Mo's last summer, fuck man, you're the luckiest mofucka I know."

"Bro, that threesome last year was fucking random, that shit don't happen all the time."

"So, what happened?"

There was a pause.

"Don't tell me you and Trace hooked up with both of them?"

"You gotta listen to the whole story, why you always jumping to the end."

"So y'all did fuck em."

"We did, but the point of the story is not that we did, the point of the story is that when it was time for us to leave, you believe this motherfucka started lobbying to stay."

"What? That's some bitch shit."

"Bro, that's what I said."

"Isn't he like your fucking rockstar cousin?"

"Right? Brooklyn be turning people into fuckbois man."

"So you left him there?"

"Yeah, I didn't want to get into it with him."

"That's so whack bro."

"Tell me about it."

Chapter Forty-Eight

In Brooklyn everyone is an artist. Everyone is an entrepreneur. Everyone is a Brand. Everyone is an enterprise. Everyone is broke. Everyone is a party. Everyone is a hustler. Everyone is about to make it big. And chances are they won't but they are trying. There are more artists in Brooklyn than any other place on the planet, and the question is always why?

After his foursome with Trace, Marla and Maria, Brenton hurried over to The Brooklyn Moon. He was meeting this young lady who produces a black burlesque show.

Brenton was unsteady. He was still pissed that Trace had stayed with Marla and Maria. He got a rum and coke and sat quietly fuming.

He looked up from his glass and saw a woman who had to be at least six feet tall standing in the doorway, looking lost. Her eyes darted around the room. She had to be Blaire. He hurried from his seat to meet.

"Hey, I'm guessing you're Blaire."

"Yes, how are you?"

"Good, could be better. And you?"

"Life is amazing."

"I like the sound of that, I might start using that."

"You're funny."

They both laughed. They felt like old friends. They sat down at a table, their conversation was easy.

"Tell me about this event," Brenton clicked into business mode.

"I can't explain it to you, you have to see it for yourself."

He waved the waiter over. They ordered a few drinks; *and Bang*.

Brenton's getting out of an Uber in front of Highline Ballroom. He's shocked by the crowd. Everyone on line is dressed semi-formal. He felt underdressed even though he was only here to scout the event.

Brenton heads up the stairs in his sly gait. He enters the main hall and stops to absorb what he had just walked into. He had just walked into a world he could not believe existed. Why did he not know about this? He knew all the goings on in NYC. Why didn't he know of this place?

Everything in the room exuded sex or sexy. A half-naked woman is on stage getting painted. Bare-chested men and masked women are walking around feeding lollipops to the patrons. The music is perfect, a nice sexy throbbing sound pushing out into the dark spaces. Everybody is beautiful. Everyone is scrumptious. The volume of all his senses moved up a few notches.

He looked across the room and saw an old friend standing by the bar, what the fuck? He thought to himself.

He went over to his friend while scanning the room for Blaire. She was nowhere to be found. He exchanged pleasantries with his old friend.

"How long have you known about this place?"

"I've been coming here for three years bro."

"Three years?"

"Yeup."

"How did you hear about it?" Brenton was shocked by the fact that this dude who was not in the business knew about this show before him.

"Someone invited me a few years back, it was a great time so I kept coming back."

Brenton could not explain why he was mad at himself, and just then he saw someone who might have been Blaire but he was not sure.

She floated over to him as if she was some supernatural being. The bar was crowded, the room kept getting tighter and tighter.

The sexual energy was slowly increasing.

Everyone was a sex god. Every drink was an elixir to cure all the banalities of life.

"So, this is what I mean when I say I can't explain it," Blaire gestured like a magician.

Brenton looked around, he was overwhelmed. He was in love. This was it. This was what he wanted to do. Yeah KEV was cool and all but he was over that part of his live. This place he was standing in was his new mission.

"I love it. I wanna work with you. I want to help you take this to the world," his mind was a buzz-saw, he was thinking about all the venues where he could get her show booked.

Blaire could tell he was sold, "Let's drink to that."

They clinked their glasses and the rest of the night was bedlam.

The performances were soaked in sexy, and shouts, and wanting, and abstract emotions about love and loss and laugher and fun and games and lights and smoke, and shots, and hugs, and lap dances, and singing, and more alcohol, and more screams, and music and chaos. The room tilted this way and that way and in the end Brenton was made a better person for it all.

Chapter Forty-Nine

Maurice has an addictive personality. He knew it. For most of his adult life he was addicted to risks and adrenaline. He had never sat down and thought about why.

It was disarming when Maybeline asked, "Why do you think we've spent this much time together."

"I don't know? It's a different time. When I first met you I thought it was gonna be a one night thing."

"Shit, that's what I thought too," Maybeline was basking in the little bit of sunlight left outside.

"Why do you think we been spending this much time?" Maurice wanted to know what she thought.

He looked at her face pressed against his chest as she spoke. She was not particularly beautiful but something about her confidence was alluring.

"I think you just fell into some good pussy and you can't get out."

Maurice laughed, she had hit the spot. He knew it and she knew it.

"You might be right," he said quietly.

"Might?" She laughed.

The glint of her gold tooth caught the light coming through the window. Maurice tried to change the subject.

"What happened to your son?"

"The young one?"

"There's more than one?"

"Yeah, I have two sons."

"I remember the one who was here the first time I came over."

"Yeah, that's Greg, and my older son is in to rap music."

"Rap music?"

"He kinda famous too," Maybeline said longingly.

"What do you mean kinda famous?"

"You heard of KEV?"

"Yeah, that's my people's artist," Maurice said out loud, by accident.

Deep down he said, *OH SHIT!*

"So you do know him? See I told you he was famous," Maybeline was proud of her son even though she had not spoken to him in six years.

"When was the last time you saw him?"

She looked off into the distance, "it's been a while."

Maybeline slid her hand under the cover and reached for Maurice's dick, "let's talk about something else."

Maurice smiled and pulled her closer.

"You know what I want you to do?" Maybeline seductively passed her hand across Maurice's chest.

"What?" He was excited.

"Fuck me raw," she was all teeth.

Maurice looked at her with narrowed eyes, "You not worried about getting pregnant?"

"Not a chance in hell, dem tubes are tied, baby."

Maurice slid the condom off and went to work.

Chapter Fifty

A text message landed in Max's phone. He was lounging at home watching Netflix. It was Thursday and he was supposed to go meet Brenton at Bed Vyne for drinks but in the meantime he would watch some meaningless drivel.

AMANDA: Just a heads up, I will be meeting with Sophie on Saturday at y'alls place. Just wanted you to know.

MAX: Thank you for the heads up. I will make sure I am not here.

AMANDA: but it would be good to see you.

MAX: Amanda, NO!

AMANDA: what are you doing Saturday evening between seven and ten?????

Max did not want to continue this conversation. He knew what Amanda was up to. He needed to quit her. He needed to quit her cold turkey.

MAX: Amanda we need to stop doing this.

His text said one thing but his dick was not having it. His dick was lobbying the rest of his body, *WE NEED THIS!*

Amanda felt her heart break a little in her chest. She needed a different plan of attack.

AMANDA: I agree with you, let's NEVER do what we did last week again. It's just that I keep thinking of you deep inside of me, and with no condom, oh my god. That was the best anyone had EVER fucked me in my life.

MAX: Amanda stop.

She knew she had him exactly where she wanted him. So she clicked into warp speed.

AMANDA: Remember that time last summer when you came over here and fucked me without even saying hello? YOU should come do that RIGHT NOW.

The text landed and max's phone got hard. He knew what was the right thing to do but knowing what is right and doing what is right, does not always make one do what is right.

Max threw his phone off to the side on his couch and walked around the apartment for a few moments. All he could think about was

how he felt when Amanda started crying when
they were at Aloft Brooklyn.

Chapter Fifty-One

Max is walking briskly down the few short blocks to Amanda's house. The entire time he is walking, he is split between two minds. One telling him to turn back and one telling him to push on.

He gets to the door. He turns the nob. It's open. His blood is filled with adrenaline and all different kinds of chemicals. His body is vibrating. He is having sexual shivers. His dick is screaming like a demon; *and Bang*.

Amanda is riding Max like she is possessed. Max is between dimensions. His dick is the rock of Gibralta and Amanda is a thousand years of torrential rain. At one point it was as if Max had totally disappeared and Amanda was just having an internal conversation with his dick. The sound of him plunging in and out of her with her juices flying every which way, was a carnal festival.

Amanda's body locked up. She was frozen with her mouth open as wide as she could. She broke out into a fit of tears as she came. Max got harder, and sploosh, his lap is filled with liquid. There is squirt juice everywhere.

Amanda is still crying, he is getting harder. Her insides are still holding-on to him. Max looks up at her crying. She has one hand over her mouth and the other pressed against his chest. He continues thrusting upward with a vengeance. His eyes tighten as he is overpowered by the most intense orgasm he has ever had.

He sat back on the couch breathing aggressively. His brain was racing, *Fuck. Fuck. What the fuck had he done?* Amanda was still sobbing. She was still straddled across his lap. He was still hard inside her.

"We gotta stop doing this Amanda."

"I know, I know, it's just that."

Max grabbed her mouth, "did you hear that?"

"What?"

Someone was trying to open her front door. They both jumped up in a hurry. Max was praying that it was not Maurice. Amanda was hoping that it was Maurice.

Chapter Fifty-Two

"How did you get out?" Max and Brenton were sitting by the bar in Bed Vyne. The bartender, Diana, had just placed two glasses of craft beer in front of them.

"I have no idea," Max said flatly.

"What?" Brenton was bewildered.

"All I know is Maurice came into the house and walked past Amanda and went straight to the bathroom. Did not event say a word to Amanda. I was hiding in the living room. Amanda stood in the hallway to block Maurice's view. So, I slid out behind her, and just like that, I was out."

"Dude, I thought you said that whole shit was done man."

"It was, I don't know what the fuck is wrong with me. I tried but for some reason she keeps texting me."

"Dude, Really?" Brenton could not believe that was his excuse.

"I know that's not a real excuse but it's all I got at the moment, I know I'm trifling," Max admitted.

"You still giving her that A dick?" Brenton looked at him sideways, "I told you about that."

"I know, I know," Max was defeated.

"Why don't you just block her?"

Max took a long gulp of his beer. He needed to schedule a session with his therapist. He liked talking to Brenton about what was happening, but more and more he was realizing that he needed professional help.

"Listen man, just fucking block her."

"You know what, I'll do that."

He had finally found a solution to Amanda but he had not found a solution his problem. He knew deep down that she had no real power over him unless he gave in to her.

Chapter Fifty-Three

"I need a huge favor," Meghan sounded desperate.

"What do you need?"

"I normally don't do this but I really need this."

"Just let me know what you want Meg." Brenton had not spoken to Meghan in over a year so it had to be an emergency for her to call him.

"I need to borrow some money," she had tears in her voice.

"I got you, I got you, how much we talking about?" Money was not an issue for Brenton he had been doing pretty well since KEV took off.

"I need like," she hesitated, "like five thousand."

She was hoping he would say yes.

"No problem, when do you need it? I can get it to you today," he said in one joined sentence.

"Today would be great," she felt her body release all its anxiety.

"You still on Classon?"

"No, I'm in Crown Heights."

"Crown Heights? Wow."

"Yeah, I live with my husband, but that's over now," there was a mawkish sadness in her voice.

"You got married?"

"I can tell you the whole story when I see you, I just need to get out of here today."

Brenton pulled up in front of Meghan's building on Lincoln Place. He walked up the three flights of stairs. She was waiting in the hallway.

Brenton handed her an envelope. She thanked him profusely.

"Anything else I can help with?" Brenton knew she needed help.

"Yeah," she shook her head in a saddest way possible.

She opened the door to her apartment. Brenton looked in. There were boxes everywhere.

"Damn that's a lot of boxes."

"I know."

"I can call a moving company for you. It's much easier to just pay them to do it, save yourself the stress," as he dials a number on his phone.

"Can they come today? I need to get out of here today."

They walked into the apartment. As soon as they walked in Brenton got a flashback of the first night he hooked up with Meghan.

He was waiting for his boy to pick up on the other end.

"Yeah, I need a favor bro," he was speaking a mile a minute.

Meghan was aroused by the way he was handling the situation. He was in crisis management mode, and it was sexy.

"They'll be here in and hour," he said as soon as he got off the phone.

She hugged him, "Thank you."

His cologne slid into her psyche. She felt her nipples getting hard. She pulled away from him. Brenton felt her energy. He walked into her living room. There was a box filled with baby toys.

"What are those?" He pointed at the box.

"Those are for my son."

"Your what?" He made the most ridiculous face he had in his repertoire.

"My son, I never told you, ah sorry, yeah I had him in February."

"Damn, you got married and had a kid in a year, that's insane. Not insane like crazy, sorry I meant that's amazing."

"You wanna see him?"

"He's here?" Brenton sounded as if she was about to show him a baby dinosaur.

"Yes, he's sleeping in the bedroom."

They walked into the bedroom and there in a tiny blue bassinet was a baby, a real baby, breathing slowly with not a care in the world.

The hairs on the back of Brenton's neck stood up as soon as he saw the baby's face. He felt like he had seen that baby before. He felt as if he had met the baby in a past life. How does he know this baby? He went through all the files in his head, he went through all his dreams, all the people he had ever met and for some reason he could not make the match. The feeling stayed with him the entire evening.

The movers came. They packed all of Meghan's things and moved her back to her old apartment where her sister was now living. Brenton hung around to make sure Meghan was situated. Her sister kept asking him if they had ever met.

"No, we have never met. Ok."

"But you look so familiar."

"I get that a lot."

"I'm so serious I feel like I know you. Do you party at Casablanca?"

"Nope," Brenton wanted her to get off the subject.

She walked away with a quizzical look on her face. Brenton walked out of Meghan's apartment with one thing on his mind. The baby. How did he know this baby?

Chapter Fifty-Four

On Friday's during the summer Bed Vyne is the red carpet at the Oscar's. Ubers pull up and Brooklyn's finest step out like stars.

Bed Vyne is a post-modern juke joint, except there is no live band. On Fridays the crowd swells out the door and onto the sidewalk. Every shade of Brooklyn shows up. At a glance it looks like the ground floor of any old brownstone in Brooklyn. But the low ceilings give it an intimacy that is captivating. The beer and wine only menu gives it an air of rustic sophistication.

Max and Sophie were on the dance area focused on each other. Emily and Brenton were locked into each other at the bar, they had been pre-gaming since 8pm. It was now midnight so they were pretty saucy. The music was like magic. People were throwing shapes left and right. The room stirred with a beautiful kind of chaos.

Trace pushed into the room with Maria and Marla like a bandit. When they walked in the room felt their presence. Trace had a hint of arrogance in his walk. He squeezed through the crowd and ordered drinks then headed to the back of the room.

He stopped to say hello to Emily and Brenton. Brenton was unimpressed.

"What's up mate?" Trace said cheerfully.

"I'm good, how bout you? You look like you doing well," Brenton looked him up and down.

"Hey Emily, this is Marla and her friend Maria from Miami," Trace gestured toward the two women.

"Brent, you know Marla right?"

"Yeah."

"And Maria?"

"No, not really."

Maria shook his hand and played along.

"Let's go dance."

Emily dragged Brenton to the overcrowded dance area. Trace followed.

Trace was trapped in a sandwich having the time of his life. The Dj switched to reggae and the room screamed.

No, no, no
you don't love me
and I know now...

The entire room erupted into singing. All the sticky sweat and wanting that was outside playing in the summer heat, came in and gyrated against everything and everyone.

Trace looked over Marla's shoulder and saw Vanessa talking to Max and Sophie. His entire life fell apart. He lost interest in Marla and Maria. He had to make his move. How was this going work? He gently slid out from between Marla and Maria.

"I'm going to the bar. Do y'all need another drink."

They both nodded yes. Marla was delivering a steady helping of grinding to Maria. Trace made a quick step towards Sophie, Max and Vanessa.

"Y'all want something to drink?"

Max knew Trace was after Vanessa but he had his own plans for the evening and Trace was not going to fuck it up.

Max raised his hand directly in front of Trace's face and said, "Nah, we good bro."

Trace was offended. Brenton saw the entire play and laughed.

"What?" Trace pretended he did not hear.

"We. Are. Good. Bro." Max tilted his head and looked him directly in his eyes.

Vanessa snickered for a bit. She remembered him from The Brooklyn Moon. He was too much. He pushed through the crowd towards the bar. Vanessa waved bye-bye. They all laughed.

Chapter Fifty-Five

It's 4 am and there are small groupings of people standing around, drunk talking. Some conversations are belligerent. Some are weedly philosophical. Some are just random words thrown together by a person too drunk to know they are too drunk. Some conversations though, were exceptionally flirtatious.

"If y'all want, we can go back to my place. I have weed and I have drinks."

"But do you have food?"

"Food? Yes. I have food at home," the bright-eyed bushy-tailed young lady said to Max, Sophie and Vanessa.

Brenton and Emily looked on. Brenton pointed to his watch. His Uber was about to arrive. They exchanged goodbyes before they headed home.

"What's the plan?" Sophie asked their newly minted friend.

Sophie loved her enthusiasm.

"Let's jump in a cab."

She pulled out her phone and like magic an Uber was there.

"I think I'm gonna head home then," Vanessa was disappointed.

"Come on, let's go hang out," Sophie pled.

Vanessa was not having any part of it. She was hoping to hang out with Max and Sophie and since that was not the case, she was going home. Vanessa walked off.

They all piled into the Uber when it arrived. Max sat in the front. Sophie sat next to Ms. Bushy-tail and her sidekick. She looked at Bushy-tail as if she was a scoop of ice cream in a lightly-warmed bowl.

"How about we make you dinner," Sophie whispered into her ear.

" Sure," her voice trembled.

Sophie smiled and looked over at her friend.

"What are you into," Sophie was trying to engage her.

She was beautiful but looked totally a-sexual.

She whispered back to Sophie, "I'm into everything."

"Are you? I feel like you're a voyeur."

"What's a voyeur?"

Sophie smiled, "Someone who likes to watch."

When they got to Ms. Bushy-tail's apartment on Jefferson, everyone had the right amount of Friday night in their blood.

The Voyeur led the way. Sophie was holding hands with Ms. Bushy Tail.

"What's your name?" Sophie asked as if she was really interested.

"Awesome." She replied looking at Sophie.

"Your mama named you Awesome?"

"Yes, she did."

"You're going to have to prove that."

And Bang.

Max and the Voyeur sat on a couch across from Sophie and Awesome. They were slowly removing each other's clothing. The room was bare. No art on the walls. No fancy homemaker set up. Just two couches, a coffee table, kitchen table and a mini bar that was stocked.

Max got up and made himself and the Voyeur a drink. They sat as if they were watching a movie. Live porn.

"What your name," Max whispered

"Grace," she whispered back.

They were trying their best not to disturb what was happening. From the look of things, Sophie was making good on her promise to make Awesome dinner. Awesome was having difficulty dealing with the amount of pleasure Sophie had in store for her.

Sophie held her in place and ate her tenderly. Awesome's eyes were like Storm from the X-men.

Max was trying his best to be a good spectator but his dick was beginning to protest.

"Sophie, do you need help?"

Sophie lifted one finger and called him over. As soon as he stood up Sophie smacked her own ass, as if to say *right here*.

Max entered Sophie from behind and immediately Grace lost her grace. She took her top off and started playing with her nipples. Then her fingers found her clit and she played a beautiful song they all enjoyed.

Chapter Fifty-Six

It was a lazy afternoon. The world outside did not exist except for the light rain against the window. Brenton and Emily are laying in bed, their legs all thrown up all over each other. Summer rain is a blessing in the city of kings.

"Yesterday, I helped an old friend move apartments and the strangest fucking thing happened." The words involuntarily droned out of Brenton's mouth.

"What do you mean?"

"Well, she had a baby who was a few months old but for some reason when I saw the baby, I felt like I had known him for years. It was so strange," Brenton stared at the ceiling.

He was searching for a thread that he could hold on to but he kept coming up with nothing.

"That is strange, how would you have known a baby?"

"That's what weird. But I know I know this baby."

Emily started laughing.

"This is serious. I swear to you it's like I met this baby in a past life or something," Brenton sat up in the bed.

Emily could see that he was really stressing over this baby. She rubbed his back gently. They went back to lazy, rainy afternoon mode.

Brenton inhaled Emily's hair and just like that he was aroused.

"This rain got me all..."

"All what?" Emily knew what he was talking about because she was having the same feelings.

He took her hand and slipped it under the covers, passing it across his erection. Emily moaned. He slipped his head below the cover and slowly kissed her neck. Then her shoulder. Then her clavicle. Then her sternum. Then her nipples. Then her navel. Then that soft area where the pelvic and hip bone meet. Emily moaned harder. He took his head from under the cover.

"You better stop playing with me," she gave him the evil eye.

Brenton smirked and went back to what he was doing. He kissed her neck; *and Bang*.

He is quietly licking juices from the edges of her extra juicy vagina. She is on her toes.

"Shhhh, relax, just breathe," he wanted her to just enjoy the moment.

God knows she tried, but he was taking his time. He was getting into apocryphal territory. She was grinding against his tongue. She could feel her orgasm building. And just as she was about to come he stopped.

"No, no, no, no, no continue, continue, continue," she pled with him.

He was waiting until he knew she would die unless he continued before he did. Then he was back at it with a more nuanced tongue and even gentler lips. She came so hard she almost crushed his skull. She was juicer than all the rivers in the world.

Chapter Fifty-Seven

"Why, would you do something like that though? These people are my family."

If Emmanuel Cox could have traveled through the phone he would have. He was hurt in a way that he did not know was possible.

"I just wanted to show you that these people do not love you, they are not as holy as you think they are," Meghan screamed into the phone.

"But, but, but that is fucking insane, do you not get that? Oh, my fucking god. You know I have to see these people all the fucking time, right?"

"That's all you care about. That's why we didn't work out? You only care about what people think of you. You don't care about me or our relationship. Those people tried to make me out to be a jezebel and instead of supporting me you sided with them," Meghan had not been this upset in a long time.

Why was she this upset? Why was she shaking?

"Babe, listen. Babe, listen," Emmanuel was hoping he could get through to her.

"How can we fix this?"

"Fix? We're done. I'm not cut out for your type of life," Meghan had closed all doors.

"What type of life are you talking about? When we met you knew what I did, right?" Emmanuel felt like he was talking to a block of steel. There was no getting through to her.

"Right?" He repeated.

Meghan was transported to the office of Rev Tatum in Atlanta. She felt his finger on her inner thigh spreading them wider and wider before he took a mouthful of her throbbing clit.

Then she was in Reverend Tatum's office with the church board accusing her of being a slut. According to them, she had seduced Reverend Tatum with her devilish ways. The reverend sat across from her in his most angelic posture, his disapproving and accusatory eyes were chastising her.

"Right?" Emmanuel was waiting for an answer.

"I knew," she said quietly.

And for the first time she realized she kept having the same kinds of relationships because she was always trying to prove that her younger self was right. She started crying. Emmanuel could hear her.

"What's going on Meghan? Where are you? Let me come get you."

"No, I don't think we'll ever work."

"Why? Why won't it work? I'm willing to make this work Meg. I'm here for you. I want to be here for you."

"It just won't E," she hung up the phone.

Chapter Fifty-Eight

Daren and Tom are back Mo's. They are right below the DJ Booth. Daren is making the shots in front of him disappear. Tom is trying to make sense of what he's explaining.

"Remember that girl Sheila?"

"Yes, the one that bought us all those drinks."

"Yes, her."

"She was cute," Tom exaggerated the last word.

"That's beside the point, oh god, can you just listen for a second."

"Ok, I'm listening. I'm listening."

"So last summer we were out partying..."

"I figured you knew her for a while," Tom cut in again.

"Can you just listen?" Daren was getting frustrated.

"I'm listening," Tom just wanted Daren to get to the point.

"Have you ever done anything crazy when you were drunk?" Daren did not know how to explain his situation to his best friend. He took another shot.

"I have only done crazy things when I was drunk, Daren," Tom said playfully.

"No, I mean crazy, crazy. Crazy like, what the fuck is wrong with me? Crazy."

"Ahhhhhh, yes. You mean like fucking a stranger in the bathroom crazy?"

"No, crazier."

"You mean like fucking someone for money, crazy?" Tom made a face like that was the craziest thing he had ever done.

"Not that crazy," Daren pulled away from Tom.

Tom was a little embarrassed.

"Ok, so listen, last summer we were hanging out here and I was drinking a lot. I mean she was buying so I was drinking a lot."

"Did y'all make out?" Tom put his hand over his mouth.

"No," Daren said dryly.

Tom was confused, "Then what's the issue?"

"She's pregnant," Daren whispered.

"Since last year?"

"No, idiot. She's pregnant now."

Tom was still confused, "That means you had sex with her? Last month! Oh shit! After I left y'all here?"

Daren's face fell, "Yeah, I was drunk."

"Drunk? Drunk? You fucked a girl?"

"That's what I was trying to explain to you."

"That you're not gay?"

"No idiot, I am gay."

"But you've been having sex with this girl for a year," Tom's tone changed.

"Ok, listen. That's not what happened, so we gon' just have to zip that up, ok. We had sex twice. That means two times. You ever hear women say they are GWI?"

"GWI? What's that?"

"Gay While Intoxicated."

"Yeah, I've heard of it," Tom had never heard of it but he wanted to see where Daren was going.

"Well, I think I might get a little bit straight when I get drunk. I don't know why. It's always been like this. I know I'm gay... but for some reason when I'm drunk, I'm a little bit attracted to women. Just a little."

"That is fucking weird Daren," Tom pulled back to look at Daren.

"Tolerance much?" Daren was put off by Tom's judgement.

"But that's different."

"No, it's not," Daren was peeved.

Chapter Fifty-Nine

Robyn is sitting on the edge of her desk. Brenton was on a small chair in front of her. She is looking her corporate best. She was wearing a dark-blue pant-suit with a crisp white button-down shirt. Brenton wanted to speak to her in person because he though she deserved that much.

"We could have done this after work, you know that right?"

"I know, but I was in the area so I figured, why not?" Brenton had been missing chances to see Robyn because he was busy having the best sex of his life. The thing about Robyn is that he did not necessarily want her for sex. He wanted her for her energy. She was in charge and something about that was a turn on.

"What do you want?" She said flirting and dismissive at the same time.

"I'm getting married."

Robyn was a little surprised, "look at you doing the right thing."

"I know, right. I just wanted to tell you in person."

"Well, I guess from now on we are just friends, right?" She was seeing if there was still an opening.

"Right," Brenton gritted his teeth.

And in that simple gesture, she knew she had one last shot at the bull-eye; *and Bang*.

Brenton and Robyn are doing things to each other they have never done before. They had only ever given each other oral. It was a strange relationship, but it worked for both of them. Robyn had an oral fixation and Brenton had something she could put in her mouth.

For the first time since they had met in the spring, Brenton was actually penetrating her.

"You have to take it easy. I don't normally have penetration sex."

"Huh. Why not?" Her breast in his mouth.

"Because I don't like giving up my power."

"Power? What Power?"

They are kissing

"I, I can't explain it without it being weird."

He is pushing into her slowly. She can feel every inch of him. It's a sweet kind of pain.

"Try me," Brenton stopped for a second, then went back to a slow deliberate stroke.

He was teasing her with the tip at this moment. She was mouth agape and moaning.

"I like sucking dick because I am totally in charge, I have you exactly where I want you. I decide when and where you come. I love that feeling," she caught her breath between each word.

Brenton looked into her eyes, "How about this?"

He went in deeper.

"Oh yes," she felt him slide all the way in. Her body started trembling.

"Stop, stop, stop, stop."

He stopped immediately.

It was too much for her. She did not want to be feeling these feeling.

She rolled him over and took his dick into her mouth with her juices smeared all over it, and took back her power. As she sucked and pumped, she slowly turned around until she was sitting flush on his face.

Chapter Sixty

Max walked all the way from is downtown Brooklyn office to The Brooklyn Moon. It was late summer and he wanted a long walk then a cold drink. He kept having thoughts about Amanda. He tried to think about other things but his mind would always end up thinking about how she squirted. He thought about the fear that raked through his body when they were almost caught by Maurice.

Amanda and Sophie are sitting in Sophie's living room. They are having wine. This was glass three or four, because nobody was counting.

"Thank you so much for working with the young women over the summer."

"It's my pleasure. I get to share my life experiences plus I get paid. I know it's not a lot but it makes me feel accomplished when I get that check," Amanda sounded extremely grateful.

"Girl stop playing," Sophie chucked her playfully.

"No, I'm serious," Amanda took another sip from her glass.

Sophie looked at her, they had had completely different lives. Amanda looked around the apartment. She thought about Max. She felt terrible knowing that she was fucking Sophie's man.

"You know what's strange?" Sophie was trying to break new ground in their friendship.

"What?" Amanda could feel her openness.

"Max and I used to argue about you," the wine was pushing Sophie into too much honesty.

"About what?" Amanda was nervous. Did Sophie know?

"I used to think that you wanted to fuck him," Sophie was frank.

Amanda almost choked, "What? Why?"

"I don't know, I was extremely jealous back then, but he would constantly tell me that I was making shit up."

"That's funny."

Amanda did not know what to do. Should she be honest and tell Sophie what had been happening?

Sophie got quiet. She looked at Amanda. Amanda looked at her.

"I'm glad we are friends now," Sophie hugged Amanda lightly.

"Me too."

"Because if we weren't friends and we did not work on this project together, I can see how, maybe we could be...," the wine stopped Sophie in her tracks.

"Could be what?" Amanda placed her glass on the coffee table, threw her right thigh on the couch and leaned forward.

"You know," Sophie said as coyly as she could; *and Bang*.

Sophie leans into Amanda. Amanda and Sophie's lips touch. They are trying their best not to be too anxious. They handle each other like they were both made out of fragile glass.

"We shouldn't," Sophie said pushing Amanda away.

"You're right, you're right."

Amanda got up from the couch and walked toward the door.

236

Chapter Sixty-One

Emily and Sheila are doing stairs in Fort Green Park. Sheila is pushing herself harder than she has ever pushed herself. Emily is happy because it made her job easier. Sheila has been her best, most dedicated client by far but today she was on a different level. She was beginning to make Emily work for her money.

Sheila paused at the top of the stairs.

"Catch up," she was in pain but she seemed to be ignoring it.

"You are in rare form today."

"I just got a lot on my mind, that's all."

"What going on?"

"Men," Sheila said with disgust.

"What happened?"

"Nothing, they're just annoying."

"This is the best way to deal with them actually, because otherwise you might end up killing someone."

"Tell me about it."

"Ok, let's do lunges," Sophie wanted to keep on schedule.

They started. Sheila stopped after a few lunges, "I'm not feeling well."

"Are you nauseous? Are you dizzy? It could be your blood sugar levels."

"No, that's not it, I'm pregnant."

"What, you're pregnant?"

"Yes, and the guy I am pregnant for does not want me to have the baby."

"That's awful.

"I know."

"What are you going to do?"

"I'm keeping it."

"Good, good for you."

Emily threw her arms around her. They hugged for a long while.

Chapter Sixty-Two

"I did it," Sheila sounded like a woman who had just lost a parent.

There was a long pause on the other side of the call. He wanted to say something but his lips would not allow him. This moment would be with him for the rest of his life. He knew it the moment her words fell on him. Daren was a different man, suddenly. He knew this was the last time he would ever speak with Sheila.

Chapter Sixty-Three

Meghan sat in the living room of her apartment on Classon, rocking her son in her arms. She felt alone but she also was basking in her new freedom. Her relationship with Emmanuel had always been a horse and pony show, she was happy it was finally over. She was forced by the church board to dress according to some standard of holiness they had developed. She hated their standards. She hated them all.

It all came to a head two nights ago when Sister Fabiola Ransom asked everyone to hang around for a special surprise she had for Meghan's birthday. The church had collected funds for a cake and a gift.

Youth leader Jeffery Patterson came strolling out of the church kitchen with a modest cake and a smile made out of lights.

Everyone cheered. Meghan was embarrassed to say the least. She almost threw up knowing that all the people around her were pretentious. Maybe it was the way they hacked into the cake, maybe it was all the fake happiness, maybe it was the way the deacon had gently touched her hand when he handed her a slice, maybe it was the way Fabiola cleared her throat before she asked for everyone's attention, maybe it was that shit eating grin on Jeffery Patterson's face but something in side of her clicked. And what she unloaded on the church could not have come at a more inopportune time.

Everyone was clapping and cheering,

Speech!
Speech!
Speech!
Speech!

Sometimes what you ask for and what you get are not the same thing.

Meghan looked around the room. She looked at the senior pastor and had a quick flash of his thick palms grasping her ass. She could still taste the menthols on his smoky breath. Her body repulsed. She looked at Emmanuel Cox. She could tell he was happy that finally the church had embraced her.

"First, I would like to thank you all for the surprise. I honestly was not expecting anything. So, thank you. I remember the first time I came here how isolated I felt. In a way, I kinda still feel isolated. I remember the whispers, the snide remarks, the disapproving looks, " she paused and looked around the room again.

Deacon Matthews must have sensed where everything was going so he tried his best to cut her off, "That's just how people are Sister Meghan. That's just how people are."

"Let me finish," she raised her hand, "So in order to fit in I did what I had to do. But what I learned about some of the people in this congregation." She paused for effect. Everyone started panicking. What did she know?

"For example, ask Deacon Matthews how long me and him have been fucking," everyone gasped. Deacon Matthews almost passed out. His wife's mouth, hit the floor.

"Ask Fabiola, what my pussy tastes like? Yes she knows."

Fabiola grasped her pearls as if Meghan was lying. The Senior pastor's cake slid off his plate and surrendered to the floor.

"Ask, Senior Pastor Brathwaite, with his funky ass, if I was sitting on his face just this evening?"

The pastor tried to protest but she snapped back.

"Was I sitting on your face his evening, or not?"

His eyes dropped to the floor and everyone knew the answer.

The name of the feelings and emotions that ran through the small gathering was a thing that could not be named.

Meghan then looked at Emmanuel and said, "These are your friends, these are the people you put ahead of me."

She walked out like a boss and left them to put the church back into the bottle.

Chapter Sixty-Four

Everyone who was present sat at the back of the church trying to process what Meghan had just said. Emmanuel Cox was embarrassed to a point where he almost turned into a block of stone. Rodin's The Thinker was a close resemblance.

No one spoke, no one was breathing. You could hear the ants walking around, gathering tiny pieces of cake.

The deacon's wife started crying and for hours that was the only sound and the only movement audible.

Chapter Sixty-Five

Emily was quivering. After a while, she could feel gentle aftershocks coursing through her body. Brenton's face was still in her lap. He had a light glaze. Her body shuttered one last time before she pulled him from beneath the covers. She wanted him inside of her.

She kissed him, she could taste her juices on his lips.

"Hmm, delicious," she smiled as she kissed him all over his face.

He entered her gently. She moaned. He kissed her gently on the neck. He nibbled on her ear. It's not that she was not enjoying what they were doing but she wanted something else.

"Brenton," she stopped him.

He looked at her, "Huh."

"I want you to fuck me, not make love to me. I want you to fuck me like you don't know me."

Brenton was shocked. In his mind he had only thought of Emily as someone to make love to.

"You want me to fuck you?" His brows were knitted.

"Yes, fuck me like you just got out of prison."

"You sure?"

"Yes Brenton, I need you to fuck me, for real, for real fuck me. Matter of fact, I need you to hurt me."

Brenton's dick got so hard, he started quoting scriptures. He licked his lips, took a deep breath, flipped her over and fucked her like a titan.

Chapter Sixty-Six

They were barely alive when he finally ejaculated all over her back.

"Yes, yes, yes, that's how I need you to fuck me every now and then. Not every day, just every now and then."

Brenton was happy that she asked for what she wanted instead of hoping he would figure it out.

"Thank you for letting me know that," Brenton was still out of breath.

"The best thing any relationship can have is communication. Just know that if you ever want anything, and I mean anything, let me know," Emily said just before she fell asleep.

The first thing that jumped into Brenton's mind was a threesome with Robyn.

How would he start that conversation?

Chapter Sixty-Seven

The following day Brenton sat at his make-shift office at Habana Outpost. He is sipping on a frozen margarita. The sun is beautiful in the sky. Everything in Brooklyn was at peace. He went over his text message one last time before he hit send.

The Craziest Party Ever II
139 Emerson
The Penthouse
Saturday Aug. 24th, 9pm
BYOB

*Dudes can only enter
accompanied by two women

Brenton's text went to his small circle of about two hundred friends. At this point all he had to do was wait. Before he could take a sip from his margarita, his phone started pinging.

He could feel the excitement in his phone. He smiled knowing his party was about to be another one for the history books.

He took a long gulp of his drink when his phone lit up. It was a call from Meghan.

He knew exactly what she wanted. He was not going to relent though. He texted her back.

Brenton: Can't talk in a meeting."

Meghan: when you are done I have something I want you to come and help me with.

Brenton: and what might that be?

Meghan: here is a hint.

She sent him a picture of her bulbus breasts, ripe and bursting with life. Brenton could feel the inside of her through the photo; *and Bang*.

He closed his eyes as she slowly slid down the full length of his dick. His head fell back onto the back of the couch as if he was a heroin addict. She rode him slowly. This was a sacrament. This was a spiritual moment between two old friends. She turned around and faced him, straddled his thighs and decided she would end his life then and there.

As Meghan came, she grabbed his face and licked it like a juicy mango. She sat on his soft dick and rocked back and forth until he got hard again. Then she fucked him a second time and sent him on his way home. She even smacked his ass on the way out the door.

"Thanks for the donation."

Chapter Sixty-Eight

M s. Clearmont was happy to see Sophie. Above all things she was impressed by the changes in Sophie's confidence. Sophie was like an animal preying on the entire world. She was always awake, always ready to pounce.

"What's new with you Sophie?"

"What new? What new?" She was toying with Ms. Clearmont.

"I had a threesome with Max and this girl we both know."

Did she just say Max? Ms. Clearmont thought to herself.

"Interesting. What was the experience like?"

"It was a little different, I was able to be myself with Max as long I was someone else with our friend. It was as if I was having a foursome, it was two of me and both of them. It was so thrilling."

"Did you and Max speak about it after?"

"Not really, No. We just kinda laughed at how mundane it all seemed."

"What about the other person?"

"She, she had the time of her life."

"How do you know that?"

"I can tell these things."

"Was there anything you did not like about the experience?"

Sophie paused for a moment. She did not want to show this side of herself. She pursed her lips.

"I got a little bet jealous during."

"Jealous, why?"

"I don't know. I'm trying to figure it out. And it was not like anything out of the ordinary happened. He was behind her and for some reason she said his name, and something about the way she said his name sounded very personal, and it made me jealous. Not jealous like I did not want him to be with her. But angry jealous like, you don't get to say his name like that jealous."

"Mm, why one and not the other?"

"The sex part to me is physical, it doesn't mean much to me. But the emotional part, she can't have."

"But why?"

"She is just there for our pleasure."

"But what about her pleasure?"

"She will get it, it just can't be personal."

"But why can't it be personal?"

Sophie was afraid to say. Ms. Clearmont knew she was having a breakthrough.

"Because," Sophie paused.

Her eyes welled up with water. She looked away and wiped the tear from her eye.

Chapter Sixty-Nine

Maurice was on his seventh drink. He had been sitting at the bar inside The Five Spot for two hours. He had come to a crossroads and this time he was going to make sure he took the right turn.

How was he going to do it? Maybe if he was drunk enough he would get the guts to break things off with her.

Maybeline finished up her shift and went to the back to get her things. She strolled past Maurice at the bar. He knew the drill.

"Come by in ten minutes, ok," she flashed her gold tooth.

"Ok," he half slurred.

He forgot that he needed his legs to get to Maybeline's apartment. The alcohol was a horde of marauding monsters trying to flip him upside down. He walked carefully to her apartment.

She cleaned up for him. Her breath smelling like mouthwash and wanting. Her dark red lipstick wet with anticipation.

She smiled him in. She knew he was a little drunker than usual. He sat at the table in the living room.

"How long are we gonna do this?" Maurice blurted out softly.

"Do, what?"

"You know, this," he drunk shrugged.

"Until we can't do it anymore."

Maybeline never asked for anything. She just wanted a little bit of dick whenever she wanted it, that was all there was to them.

She did care about him but not enough to impose herself on his life. She had never asked him a single word about his family. As far as she was concerned, he did not have a family.

"I think we should stop doing this."

"What happened? You can be honest with me. You know that, right?"

She was a bit horrified at the fact that she had spent a year training Maurice to hit all the right spots and now he was leaving.

"It just not working, aint' no future here," he was trying to hurt her.

He did not know how to end the relationship in a mature way.

Maybeline realized that what he was talking about had nothing to do with her per se. She shrugged.

"Ok, let's stop."

Maurice was shocked that she did not put up a fight or try to stop him from ending what they had. He was uncomfortably drunk. He did not know what to say. He had not planned for things to end this easily.

"So, I guess I will be leaving then," he said quietly.

"No the fuck you're not. You gon' have to fuck me first. And fuck me real go too." She said in her sweetest southern twang.

Maurice smiled; *and Bang*.

Chapter Seventy

Max, Sophie and Venessa are sitting in Max and Sophie's living room. They are having wine. Red. Sophie has a few pamphlets about open relationships. She hands one to Max. She hands another to Vanessa and smiles.

The sexual tension and energy could power all of New York City.

"What's all of this?" Vanessa wanted to know.

"Me and Max spoke about our last two adventures with you and we wanted to see if we can set down some basic rules."

"Rules, that sounds sexy," Vanessa said flirtatiously, her eyes trained on Sophie.

"I'm thinking you should be our pet."

"What does that mean?"

"It means we should make this official," Sophie winked on the last word.

Vanessa looked at Max. Max looked a Sophie.

"We spoke about it," Max said carefully.

"But why me?"

"Because you understand, you get us. Plus I like you."

Vanessa blushed. She reached over and touched Sophie's thigh.

"So, is there paperwork to be signed?" Vanessa said jokingly.

They all burst out laughing.

"Actually yes, there is," Sophie said holding back her laughter.

"Oh," Vanessa was surprised.

Sophie handed her a sheet of paper with all the rules.

Vanesssa started mouthing some of the rules in a semi-whisper, "All sexual contact has to be confirmed between all parties. All parties must be tested every three months."

She looked up at Sophie and Max.

"I'm guessing that one is for...me."

"Yes but no, we want to make sure you know that we are also safe for you."

"Condoms are a must," Vanessa kept reading.

"You don't have to sign this today, so if you wanna take it home and go over it you can."

"Whatever happens between us, stays between us," Vanessa smiled at that particular clause because privacy was important to her.

Max and Sophie watched her as she read.

"It all looks good to me."

Vanessa skimmed the rest of the document then smiled and took the pen from Sophie and signed the sheet of paper. Max and Sophie did the same.

"What now?" Vanessa asked as she emptied her glass of wine.

"What now?" Sophie said searchingly.

"Let's start with another glass of wine shall we, Max got up to go get a new bottle; *and Bang*.

Chapter Seventy-One

"How have things been with you Max?"
"Things have been amazing. I'm still struggling with, you know my issues."

"What happened?"

"I relapsed."

"Relapsed?"

"Yes," Max thought about the last time he saw Amanda, "but I'm good now. I know for a fact that I am through with her."

"What happened Max?" Ms. Clearmont said in an overly concerned voice.

"I almost got caught in a situation that was so insane, I'm just happy I made it out alive.?"

"What happened?"

"Her husband came in while we were...," he made a face at Ms. Clearmont.

He could feel his heart beating.

"So, the reason you are stopping is not because you found the root cause of your behavior but because you see how dangerous your behavior can be."

"I wouldn't say that. I know the root cause of my behavior," Max shot back.

"You do?" Ms. Clearmont was all ears.

"Yes, I do. Besides the fact that I love having sex, I think I do it for the thrill. I think I do it because something about the idea of getting caught makes it extremely intoxicating." Max was shocked by the words that were coming out of his mouth, he was channeling Brenton.

"How did you come to this conclusion?"

He was stuck. He was honest but he was not that honest. He threw the thought around in his head.

"I think I want to get caught. I don't know why? I love the thrill of getting away with something I should not be doing. Maybe it's the narcissist in me. We all have that side. I could have cheated with anyone in the world, but I chose my best friend's wife."

He paused for a long time thinking about the horror of what he just said.

Ms. Clearmont was happily amazed. His clarity was almost arousing. If she were honest with herself, his clarity turned her on a little bit.

"Well, I must say I have never seen anyone get to where they needed to get as fast as you have, well done Max."

Max walked out into the dreamy August sun like a man freed from his history. He took out his phone and called Sophie.

"Hey, what's up?" Sophie was overjoyed.

"I just want to let you know that I love you."

"Aww, you gonna make me cry."

"I wanna take you out to dinner tonight, what time do you get off?"

"This evening? Six. But I can leave earlier if you want."

"Six is good, I'll come and meet you out front."

Chapter Seventy-Two

The resurrected myth of the first *The Craziest Party Ever* circulated through Brooklyn like a hunger, like a shapeless spell, like a nervous ghost calling out to all those who thirst for all things epic.

Whenever there is a good party brewing in Brooklyn, all the people who need to know will know, will find out, will show up. There is a secret society of partiers in Brooklyn. The best you can hope for is that someone who is a member will invite you so that you can, or may be initiated into the circle of the party gods.

To be in the circle one has to be in a constant search for beauty, for revelry, for other-worldly experience, but most of all one has to be able to throw shapes. Because what is a party without shapes. What's the point of having a brilliant DJ who knows how to get the sonics into the body without a conclave of like-minded individuals who are willing to open the body like an instrument, who are willing to make a joyful noise unto the entire history of sound making.

Brooklyn was quiet because everyone was sharpening their bodies for what was guaranteed to be the craziest party ever.

Chapter Seventy-Threer

That evening the sun blew it's last good-bye kiss to the county of kings and threw colors in the sky that were a promise of the magnificent Saturday that was brewing. Brooklyn felt like saffron flavored memories trapped in an old sepia photograph.

Brenton walked around his apartment making sure everything was in place. His alcohol table was looking pretty impressive for a BYOB party.

He walked out onto the roof deck. Everything was perfect. There were lounge furniture and chairs from different walks of life. His new grill sat watching like a roman centurion. He smiled, he knew the mayhem of flavors that was about to take place on that grill. He thought about inviting Meghan. He copied the text he had sent to everyone and sent it to her.

There was a knock at his door. It was the DJ. He was an hour early. for Brenton that was a very good omen. DJs are never early. It was DJ Big Phenom and his fellow traveler DJ Mega. They stood in the doorway covered in sweat, looking like Donkey and Shrek.

Brenton pointed them to the spot where they were to set up. In about twenty minutes they were done and they started playing mood music.

"We bout to go get something to eat down the block bro," Big Phenom informed Brenton.

"Just be back before nine."

"Bet," they said in unison.

Chapter Seventy-Four

The DJ was back by eight-forty-five and started spinning like it was two in the morning. He had made a promise to Brenton that he would keep the party jumping all night. Folks started showing up a little before nine.

It seemed the theme was exotic bottle party. Everyone through the door brought bottles extracted from their sacred stashes. A bottle of something sacred at a BYOB party is an overture of one's commitment to the finer things and one's willingness to share said fineries.

Within an hour the living room, the kitchen and both bedrooms were crowded. The living room was the main dancefloor which was on fire. The Bedrooms were the chill areas, but for the moment they served as drug dens and private dance rooms.

The myth of what happened last year was trying to outdo itself. A group of women showed up in all see through tops. Dudes started taking their shirts off as a show of solidarity. The bedroom closest to the patio was one thick slice of weed fog. Someone was walking around the party handing out edibles. Why would someone be giving out free edibles at a party? No one knows but it was provocative.

Every song the DJ played was a chance to sing along. The living room was a gospel choir, the bedrooms were brothels, the roof patio was a suicide note. The view of Manhattan was a scene from some mystic city in outer space.

As the troops poured in, the carnal nature of the party swelled exponentially. The throbbing bass line was clawing at the core of the people on the dance floor. So, when the DJ decided to start playing reggae, it was as if Jesus just snatched the nails out of his hands and feet and climbed off the cross. Everybody's motions could only be explained with complex graphs, charts and equations used to land objects on Mars.

The DJ stopped mid-song and the room hollered. He knew what he was doing. He wanted them to beg for it. When he dropped the beat. The hounds of hell were unleased. People were whining through each other. Legs and arms and hips and faces and tongues and shoulders and butts and thighs spoke in languages only familiar to other body parts.

 Daren showed up dressed like a seventies film star. He was draped by a shiver of Somali models even finer than the ones he came with the year before. Where did he find these models? Only god knew. His friend Tom was dressed like a tiny white pimp.

Daren was focused on finding KEV. He headed straight to the smoke room. He was not prepared for the level of whinery he witnessed. Some random dude in the smoke room offered him MDMA. And being Daren, he accepted it.

Tom and the Somalian models went to the drink table. They placed their small cavalry of bottles amongst the city of bottles that were already there.

Max, Sophie and Vanessa arrived at eleven. They were not expecting this many people this early. They could barely squeeze through the crowd. The roof deck was filling up. The hallway by the elevator was getting crowded.

Max took their bottles to the drink table. Vanessa and Sophie started dancing. Max felt left out. He went to find Brenton. Brenton was on the roof deck flirting with Emily. He was lit.

"Bro, how many people did you invite?"

"All of them."

"What's up Emily."

"Hey Max," she was also lit.

"The hallway is packed bro, people can't make it through the living room."

"There's tons of space out here."

He looked around the roof deck.

"Yeah but they can't get through the living, and the music is not really getting out here."

"Give me a second."

Brenton ran off.

A few moments later the DJ was stringing wires through the window and setting up speakers on the roof deck.

People poured onto the roof deck as soon as this happened. Maybe it was the free edibles or the MDMA, or maybe it was the fresh air but a new kind of festive madness was in everybody.

The DJ stopped the music for a second and said something about getting warmed up before he dropped the latest Soca hit and folks almost started jumping off the roof.

Chapter Seventy-Five

Max went back into the living room. Sophie and Vanessa were nowhere to be found. He went into the chill room. They were sitting next to a dude dressed like a space pirate. They introduced him.

"So you're just giving out free MDMA?"

"Yeup."

"But why?"

"It's a party right?"

"True."

Max had a little and they all went back to the living room.

When KEV got off the elevator there were whispers. People were surprised to see him at a house party. KEV loved the feeling of people watching him, of people talking about him. The crowd parted for him and his small harem. As soon as he got into the house he ran into Daren.

"Not now ma dude," he froze out Daren.

Daren's heart rolled out of his chest onto the dance floor. He would spend the rest of the night looking for it.

By midnight there was no place left for people to fit. They started moving into the stairwell. Someone started playing Spotify on their phone and a second party evolved.

There was no way of knowing how many people were at the party. The only thing that was sure, was that people kept texting friends and telling them to come by.

The person who was buzzing people in stopped. If you did not live in the building you could not enter.

Trace came to the party with Victoria. But spent most of the night trying to get Vanessa's attention. When he finally got her attention, he pulled her to the side.

"I know you might not remember me, but..."

"I do remember you," she touched his chest.

"I've been meaning to ask you to grab a drink with me or something, if you are ever free," he looked into her eyes.

She gazed back in his eyes. He knew they had a connection. She licked her lips and smiled at him. She passed her hand across his chest again. Victoria saw it all. She was steaming.

"You know I'm here with Sophie and Max, right?" Vanessa could feel the MDMA in her blood. She wanted to touch someone. She wanted some water.

"Yeah, I know but I'm trying to like really, really see you."

"Ha, you are funny. You have zero chance of seeing me, especially since you are friends with Max. What kind of a friend are you?" She walked off.

Trace watched her as she walked away.

"You motherfucker," Victoria screamed into his ear.

Chapter Seventy-Six

At two in the morning, the lights went from black to red. The room was one giant orgy of gyration. The DJ was playing nineties R&B. Then Prince came through the speakers.

I wanna be your lover...

Everyone started singing at the top of their lungs.

Brenton was surprised when he saw Meghan at the party.

"Hey you came."

"You know I wouldn't miss this party for a million dollars," they both laughed.

Meghan spotted Sophie. She headed over to say hello. Brenton thought about Meghan's son. Who did the baby remind him of? Why did he know her baby?

Max and Sophie introduced Meghan to Vanessa. They were laughing and smiling for a bit before Sophie dragged Meghan off into the bathroom. They closed the door behind them and started whispering.

"Who's that Vanessa girl?"

"She's cute right?"

"Cute? She is fucking amazing, who is she?"

"You are not going to believe this."

"What?" Meghan did not know what to expect but she was excited.

"She's our pet."

"Your what?"

"Our pet, like our girlfriend."

"Hold on." Meghan tried to process what she had just heard. she was hurt for the obvious reason. Why didn't Sophie ever ask *her* to be their pet. She pretended to be happy.

"That's, that's amazing Sophie."

"I know, right?"

They were quiet for a second. Meghan thought about the last time she hooked up with Sophie. She could feel Sophie's fingers gently calling her through her g-spot. Her panties got wet immediately.

"I have to go get a drink."

"No stay, what has been happening with you."

Sophie wanted to talk. She wanted to touch somebody and Meghan was the perfect candidate. She slid her hand over Meghan's shoulder.

"I just moved back in with my sister at the old apartment."

"What? Why?" Sophie was still rubbing her shoulder.

Meghan could barely speak. This was too much. Meghan went in for a kiss. Sophie was caught off guard.

"Meghan, what are you."

"Shhh," she placed one finger on Sophie's lips.

"We can't, we can't, we can't, not right now Meg," Sophie could feel Meghan's sadness, but she knew this was not the time or place.

Chapter Seventy-Seven

The Party hit the final stretch at around four in the morning. The DJ was playing like he owned three planets. He was playing pop songs that were closely partnered with the alcohol that was stumbling through the blood of the party. The dronage was peaking. Everything was right in the universe. The chill room was two thirds orgy and four fifths lap dance cathedral. Brenton was on the roof deck smoking with a group of white kids from Bushwick.

"Whose party is this?" Everyone was speaking louder than they should.

"This is my party man," Brenton was holding on to Emily, "me and my lady threw this party man."

"Get out bro," they were happy to be sharing their smokes with the party host.

"How did ya'll hear about the party?"

"Someone posted a video on facebook."

"On facebook? What? Did ya'll get something to drink?"

"Earlier, yes."

Brenton walked off with Emily toward the living room. The living room was a hive of shapes filled with ritual magic and rhythmic overload. It was a museum of desperation and swag. It was a cross between loneliness and forever. If Brooklyn was a corpse, this party was a bouquet of flowers blooming out of its mouth.

It was impossible to enter the living room without turning into a rhombus or a triangle. Daren was in the middle of the dance floor surrounded by his shiver of Somali models. He was having the time of his life. KEV stood by the chill room door watching him.

Max, Vanessa and Sophie were one person on the dance floor. It was as if the music had glued them together.

Brenton ordered sandwiches from Farmer in the Deli through Uber eats.

The party was slowly winding down. Brenton asked the DJ to play chill out music.

Folks started heading back to their empires.
They left filled all the way up to their eyeballs.

Chapter Seventy-Eight

The sandwiches arrived at five. The sun was showing its fingertips by then. The skyline was a deep reddish-orange.

Brenton was looking at the skyline. He wondered where Emily was. He looked around for her. Max came onto the roof with Sophie and Vanessa close behind him holding hands. They were still in party mode.

"You seen Emily?

Max thought for a second, "Yeah, she's in the chill room talking to some dude."

Brenton was drunk so he was talking slower than normal. He was wobbling on his feet.

"Did you see Meghan?"

"Yeah, earlier tonight," Max was still coming up, so he hugged Brenton to help him balance.

"I, I went to help her move the other day."

"You did? Where did she move to?"

"She moved back to her old place, with her sister."

The DJ turned the music off and started packing up.

"And she had a, hold on," Brenton reached into his pocket.

He showed Max a tiny box.

"Is that a fucking ring?"

"Shhh, don't speak so loud."

"That's for Emily?"

"I'm gonna ask her to marry me."

"When?"

"I was gonna do it tonight but look at me."

"Yeah, do it another time bro."

"I know, right?" Brenton smiled.

Max kept him on his feet. He walked him over to a lounge chair that had just opened up. They both sat. Sophie and Vanessa were dancing to no music.

"So, did you know Meghan had a bady?"

"She did? When?" Max was shocked.

"This year, but you know what's weird when I saw her baby I felt like I had met her baby before..."

As soon as the words came out of Brenton's mouth he was fully sober. He had never been more sober or clearer in his life. He had a flashback to the first moment he saw Meghan's baby. All his thoughts crashed into his head like a pile up on an icy highway.

"Oh Shit, Max," he grabbed Max's face and looked into Max's soul with the widest eyes possible, "the baby looks exactly like you bro."

the end.